# Passarola Rising

VIKING

# Passarola Rising

## AZHAR ABIDI

VIKING
Published by the Penguin Group
Penguin Group (USA) Inc., 375 Hudson Street, New York, New York 10014, U.S.A. • Penguin Group (Canada), 90 Eglinton Avenue East, Suite 700, Toronto, Ontario, M4P 2Y3 Canada (a division of Pearson Penguin Canada Inc.) • Penguin Books Ltd, 80 Strand, London WC2R 0RL, England • Penguin Ireland, 25 St. Stephen's Green, Dublin 2, Ireland (a division of Penguin Books Ltd) • Penguin Books Australia Ltd, 250 Camberwell Road, Camberwell, Victoria 3124, Australia (a division of Pearson Australia Group Pty Ltd) • Penguin Books India Pvt Ltd, 11 Community Centre, Panchsheel Park, New Delhi - 110 017, India • Penguin Group (NZ), Cnr Airborne and Rosedale Roads, Albany, Auckland 1310, New Zealand (a division of Pearson New Zealand Ltd) • Penguin Books (South Africa) (Pty) Ltd, 24 Sturdee Avenue, Rosebank, Johannesburg 2196, South Africa

Penguin Books Ltd., Registered Offices: 80 Strand, London WC2R 0RL, England

First published in 2005 by Viking Penguin, a member of Penguin Group (USA) Inc.

10   9   8   7   6   5   4   3   2   1

PUBLISHER'S NOTE
This is a work of fiction. Names, characters, places, and incidents either are the product of the author's imagination or are used fictitiously, and any resemblance to actual persons, living or dead, business establishments, events, or locales is entirely coincidental.

LIBRARY OF CONGRESS CATALOGING-IN-PUBLICATION DATA
Abidi, Azhar
   Passarola rising / Azhar Abidi.
      p. cm
   ISBN 0-670-03465-7  (alk. paper)
   1. Jesuits—Fiction. 2. Flying-machines—Fiction. 3. Portugal—History—John V, 1706–1750—Fiction. I. Title
PR9619.4.A25P37 2006
823'.91—dc22      2005042430

Printed in the United States of America
Set in Elysium with Escrita
Designed by Carla Bolte

FOR KAREN

# Passarola Rising

# { 1 }

ON THE twenty-seventh day of the month of June, in the year of grace 1731, my brother, Bartolomeu Lourenço, rose on his airship from the ancient ramparts of São Jorge Castle. I remember the day as clearly as if it were yesterday. There was a smattering of clouds in the sky, like bands of white lace dyed orange by the sunset. The weather was pleasant. A gentle breeze blew in from the sea, bringing with it the occasional whiff of seaweed. My brother tied a rope to the bow of the airship and tethered its other end to a stake in the ground. He walked with me to the ship, with a solemn and measured gait. His yellow pointer, Sacha, lapped at his feet. The sleek vessel seemed as large as a seagoing sloop. A vacuum pump roared and the rope pulled taut. I climbed a rope lad-

1

der lowered from the deck and looked back over the bulwarks. The airship rose three or four feet from the ground. Bartolomeu held the rope tight for a moment. We looked at each other. He was a tall, slim man of twenty-six, with arctic-gray eyes and golden blond hair. I was nineteen years old.

"Ready to explore the sky?" he asked.

I nodded.

"Frightened, yes?"

"No . . . not I."

"Excellent!" he shouted and leapt inside.

He drew his sword and with one swift motion untied the moorings. The *Passarola* rose, spinning like a top as it gained height. We edged past the towers and came to float some hundred feet above the castle. Below us we could see the royal gathering: there stood His Majesty João V, clapping his hands with glee; an astrologer had told him that he would lead Portugal to a new age of exploration. Next to him stood the Duke of Aveiro, my brother's patron and uncle of my beloved, waving his tricorne with an expression of relief on his face. Beside him was his lovely niece Maria, a rosebud among nettles. A little apart stood Cardinal Conti, watching us with his murderous stare, and other courtiers with their mouths agape. Some of them waved, others shouted, "Bravo!" but the Cardinal, a towering presence in white, only crossed himself.

The *Passarola* began to climb. Now I could see the entire estate, the church and pastor's residence to my left and the castle below me. Next to it were the barns, the stables, the armory turned into a brewery and the houses for the workers. I then saw the fields, like a chessboard of green and golden squares draped over the hills. The potato farmers were returning home. The shepherds were flocking their cattle into the pens. The squat peasant women were herding their children. I could hear every sound: the cries of babies, the church bell ringing, the sheepdogs barking. The land glowed at the horizon. The sky where the sun had sunk was burnt red. The seven hills were lit with its last rays. The trees were full of chirping birds but their sounds grew fainter by the minute. Bats swept close to our heads. Now Lisbon appeared to my left, shrunk in size to a footprint, and the river Tagus itself no larger than a small stream. We lost sight of our people in the evening haze. The air was cold and except for the sound of the wind in our sails, we were surrounded by silence.

3

We hoisted the jib and mainsail and let the wind take us out toward the harbor. My senses reeled from the wild perspectives around us. I walked to Bartolomeu, who was leaning against the tiller. He smiled and shook my hand.

I felt happy for him. This was his moment of triumph. He had labored for years to perfect his flying machine but his experiments had been disasters. He had been ridiculed and threatened by the Inquisition. Poets had written satires about him and children had taunted him with cries of *O Voador*—the Flying Man. But he had persevered. He had gone hungry for his work and had confounded his critics. I could have danced in wild excitement but he merely looked weary. He filled his pipe and lit it, staring at the horizon for a long time.

"There's something I must ask of you," he finally said. "It's little that I care for my life, but if worst comes to worst and something happens to me, will you bear my witness?"

I took little notice of his words at the time because I had no reason to doubt that our future was going to be anything but splendid. Never did I imagine that I would be called upon to dust off the ship's logs and leaf through my yellowed journals to recall the events of those distant years. But in the narrative that follows, I, Alexandre Lourenço, must now—finally, and with a heavy heart—carry out that promise. ℰ

# { 2 }

OUR FAMILY was not rich but we had a comfortable life. Our father, Don Francisco Lourenço, was a surgeon. He met our mother in Lisbon, where he had gone to study medicine, and brought her back with him, like his manuals and instruments and so many other things, to Brazil.

An elegant and straight-backed man, he always wore his coat and hat when he left the house and paid no regard to the heat. It was as if he donned his cape to smite it. He left in the morning before we awoke and returned home after we had been put to bed. On the Sabbath he rose at daybreak and tended his garden with the same meticulous care, I suspect, that he applied to his patients, except that this time the malady was not malaria but weeds. In those days

6

we children used to imagine that we were not his real family because he did not show us any love. I now think that he was too absorbed in his work to be distracted by affection. It was not that he was incapable of love but he was incapable of demonstrating it until one of us was taken ill. Only then would his paternal instincts awaken and he would exclaim, "May God give me your fever!" or say to our mother, "Let him have what he wants!" or exempt us from going to school. The patient was lanced and bled, and tourniquets were applied with great care. Our father would even spend the night by a child's bedside, checking the pulse, fetching water, wiping the forehead and applying ice to the child's palms and soles when the fever broke. And in the morning we found him asleep, slumped in a chair, beside the patient's bed. Once, when I gashed my leg, I imagined that he would amputate it and keep it in a pickled jar along with his leeches. But these were fancies we entertained to keep ourselves occupied. We did not fear him. The fact was that we coaxed out of him all the sweets and toys that we could while ill because as soon as the patient recovered, father's stiffness of manner returned.

My mother never saw São Paulo as her home. For

her it was always a point of departure. She kept her belongings in trunks that she had brought along with her from Portugal: mirrors, chintz, parasols, petticoats and lace—all bought in Lisbon. I remember rummaging through them for hours as a child. They retained a smell of another time and place until, many years later, the smell of mothballs overcame it. The climate did not suit my mother. Mosquitoes bit her at night and the bright sun turned her red as a lobster. She never ventured into the forest, imagining it a green hell seething with snakes, pumas and naked cannibals. She preferred to spend—or I should say bide—her time indoors, playing baccarat with the other Portuguese ladies who also thought of Brazil as their purgatory. My mother believed that the colonies were crude places. Men ran to ruin here and women turned into whores. I used to cling to her skirts, I recall, because she was always speaking of returning to Lisbon and I feared that she would leave us with our father, who would forget to even feed us. In her mind only Europe remained a refuge. Its fine boulevards, baroque palaces and great harbors were the antidotes to the mulattoes, the flies, the heat and the forest. I suspect that as she grew older, this image of a refuge turned almost into an idea of an earthly heaven.

The desire to be elsewhere, I inherited from her.

I was the third child in a household of two brothers and two sisters. Bartolomeu was the eldest of my siblings. He left home at an early age and did what he pleased. He attended the seminary at Bahia but never embraced the convictions of the church. Ordained as a priest, he thought like a scientist. "It is harder to prove the presence of God than his absence," he would say, to the dismay and horror of his peers.

When I followed him to the seminary a few years later, I discovered that he had become obsessed with flight. It was a common occurrence around the complex to hear the bleating of a sheep or the quacking of a poor duck with no animal in sight until the shadow of a balloon with a basket dangling underneath floated past. His experiments were notorious. Once I saw the fathers watch in despair as he sent up a large balloon with a basket dangling underneath, except that this time it carried a human passenger— me. To mollify the priests, he built a system of drains, levers and pulleys to take water from the river up

9

the hill to the buildings. Later, he built a boat without oars. A windmill on top of its mast turned the blades of a wheel, propelling the boat forward and overturning all hopes of our poor parents as a plow turns the soil, proving that he could do whatever he fancied rather than follow the marked path. This was a notion which I held dear at that time. I was in awe of him, I confess, and wished to form my future under his guidance. ℰ

# { 3 }

A T THE age of fifteen, I followed Bartolomeu to Lisbon, where he had gone to live with relatives. They had friends at the Portuguese court and thanks to their good offices, I obtained the position of a court page. Although a post of little distinction, it opened doors for those who were prepared to flatter and charm their way through the ranks. However, courtly duties were not suited to my temperament and I soon fell into a lethargy. I was neither cunning nor ambitious, and the court had nothing to offer me. My only motivation for staying was the beautiful Maria Veldavez, one of the ladies-in-waiting attached to the Queen. I had not had much experience with girls and was holding out my love for a lofty creature such as she—soft and fair, wearing lace gowns and ostrich feathers. Promptly I fell in love.

It was not long before I was introduced to her at a ball. I had been dreaming to make her acquaintance and made myself as agreeable as I could. There followed days when a glance from her would send me into a fit of wild excitement and other days when I saw her flirting with other young men and felt sick. I was convinced that fate had caused us to meet but could not understand why I was being denied her favor. She was unattainable, of course, for I was a mere page and she was the niece of the Duke of Aveiro. But I cherished the notion that she too was holding out her love for a hero. I passed my time by thinking of noble deeds that would make me worthy of her. This hope, no matter how futile, made my tenure endurable.

§

I WAS living in a hostel in those days and Bartolomeu was teaching at Coimbra. Due to our hectic lives, we seldom saw each other except for brief exchanges in the palace. By all accounts, he had established a formidable reputation as a scientist ever since arriving in Portugal. His classes at Coimbra were packed with students and the King's advisers hung on to every word he said. I suspect that he rather enjoyed the awe that he inspired for, although he was not an arrogant man, he liked to keep his own counsel. He had always been a solitary fellow. Even when we were younger, he liked to climb trees or go out into the forest to catch butterflies rather than play with other children. I used to be his occasional companion but as we grew up, he became occupied with his studies and our adventures came to an end.

I left home because all men of good households left the colonies at my age to find their fortune elsewhere. It was an old and respectable tradition but I missed home and disliked the uncertain business of growing up. It was as if leaving home had brought an end to my happy childhood and I regretted its passing. Of course, I had made the choice of coming to Lisbon because of my brother, but our lives were very different now.

It was under these circumstances, I recall, that my brother sent for me. My carriage drew up directly outside an apartment he kept in the Terreico do Paço. An old maid opened the door and, nodding silently, led me through a dark passage to his study.

He stood over a small desk, like those once used by medieval scribes for illuminating manuscripts. An assortment of dusty inkwells, like tinctures, lay arrayed on a ledge beside him.

"So, here you are!" he said, putting down his quill. "I remember when you were a little boy, playing with the mulattoes in the dust. Now look at you! Dressed up to the nines you are... all in wig and velvet waistcoat and frilled cuffs and breeches! Tell me, are you happy at your post?"

I did not wish to disappoint him and said that I was.

My brother allowed himself a faint smile. "I no longer don the cassock but don't forget that I was trained to hear confessions. If there's one thing that I've learnt, it is to watch for the ever so slight flicker of the pupils; yes, the gaze a little too steady that gives a man away. We shall not hold this against you but I've reason to believe that you tell a lie."

When I remained silent, he filled his pipe and continued. "You don't seem to have the ambition to climb the ranks. Opportunities await you but I cannot see any enthusiasm. My boy, if you're to remain here, you must, what's the word, shall we say ... mingle."

"I cannot do it," I replied.

"But why not?"

"Because it saps me," I said. "Do you know what I must do all day? I must speak in a low voice because it sounds authoritative, I must stomp my feet when I walk, I must bluster and brag to create a pretense of work and I must always be witty. I find it all quite intolerable."

He motioned for me to sit down. "I didn't call you here for rebuke," he said gently. "The court is a place for parasites and those who have hopes of gain. Your time there was well spent, mind you, for now you've seen it and it will be easier for you to turn away."

"I have not let you down?"

"Why, of course not. You are not cut for these things, I dare say, and may do better than living out your life in a daze."

I averted my glance and took a moment to cast my eyes around the room. The shelves overflowed with books by Descartes, Leibniz and Newton. More piles rose from the floor. Sheaves of notes lay scattered everywhere. A model of a cart without horses took up what spare room there was. This contraption seemingly moved by the motion of wind, which turned around a shaft, which in turn rotated the axle with the wheels attached to it. A wooden cross hanging over the door was the only reminder of his faith.

"I want to make something of my life," I said.

"And you will."

"I am afraid I won't," I replied. "I don't know what I want."

"Most people don't know what they want," he said. "They discover it. It takes time."

"I fear that I will never know," I said.

Bartolomeu smiled. "I wonder who you inherited that poetic temperament from," he said. "Not from our father, to be sure."

"I wish I had a calling," I said.

"Not everyone has a calling, Alex."

"Then what am I to do?"

"I think you and I should spend more time together."

I glanced up at him.

"You have time?" I asked.

It was a childish thing to say but he looked at me

searchingly. "Alexandre, I must be honest with you," he said.

"Well?"

"I need your help."

"For what purpose?"

A shy smile appeared on his lips. "To sail a ship that flies above the land and the sea."

I recalled the fact that several years before he had coaxed a petition from the King with the promise of an invention that would make the Portuguese masters of the air; however, the device, which was a paper globe filled with hot air, had risen perhaps ten or twelve feet before bursting into flames and threatening to set fire to the building where the performance had been held.

I shook my head in disbelief. "If you try again, you'll make a bonfire of the Casa da India," I said.

He made a clicking sound with his tongue. "No, no, no . . . they'll make a bonfire of me!"

"What do you mean?"

"They don't want me to finish building my ship."

"Who are they?"

"The Cardinal and his lot. He's written to the Vatican, saying that a certain Jesuit has built a *'corpo esferico di poco peso'* that rises to a height of *'due canne'* and that he is building another. They are watching me."

"I don't understand."

"They are afraid that I'll sail my ship through the ether and find what must not be found."

"What must not be found?"

"Perhaps that the heavens are empty and there is no God," he said with a shrug, "because if there's no God then there cannot be a religion, and without religion how will our popes, cardinals and bishops ever live off the land? That's what they must fear."

The church's reason seemed justifiable to me. "May the Lord protect us," I said. "Perhaps some truths are best left hidden."

He removed his pipe. "If there were uncharted islands across the sea and you had a ship, would you not go? Or would you believe those who tell you that they are inhabited by monsters? Fear, Alex, is our greatest enemy."

He smoked for quite a while, looking at me, then watching the smoke rise to the ceiling. "Alex, they are within a hairsbreadth of my life. I don't have much time. I am a crucified man already and my bones will be broken in the bargain. I must build my

18

machine before the Holy Office finds an excuse to arrest me."

"The King won't stand for that."

"Then you don't know the Cardinal. People who displease him meet their deaths most conveniently—they fall off cliffs, they drown, they are run over by horses or they simply disappear, vanishing into thin air, and no one dares ask any. questions. He is one of the last inquisitors who burnt witches and before he dies, he wants the hunts started again. No one interferes with him."

This talk made me fearful. "What do you want me to do?" I asked.

He unrolled a parchment scribbled with calculations and a pencil drawing of what appeared to be a seagoing yawl, with long and graceful lines to cleave through the wind without opposition. Two panels of wood, presumably leeboards, extended on either side of the hull. Two cross sections displayed the hull's interior. At the bottom of the hull was a hold where stores and provisions would be kept. The ship had two masts and three sails. The only difference between an ordinary boat and this craft was that the deck was suspended underneath four large copper spheres.

"Behold the *Passarola*!" he remarked, beaming with pride.

"Is *this* your ship?"

"It most certainly is."

"What are these?" I asked.

"Vacuum spheres."

I shook my head in wonder.

"A vacuum sphere weighs less than a similar sphere filled with air. It will rise into the air because the vacuum inside the sphere has no density compared to the air outside it. I have calculated that if each sphere is seven feet in diameter, with a thin copper shell less than one-tenth of an inch thick, then it will be almost weightless, and four such spheres would displace enough air to take account of the ship's weight and a small payload. I have also calculated the ship's dimensions. It must be fully fifty-nine feet long from stem to stern and fifteen feet wide. The forecastle, exactly twelve feet long and nine feet wide. One inch more and the ship becomes too heavy to lift into the air; one less and it is too light."

"Are the spheres capable of resisting atmospheric pressure?"

"Perfectly! They'd resist the atmosphere's pressure in the same way that an air bubble resists the pressure of water around it."

I sighed in admiration. My brother delighted in understanding how things worked and had a limitless capacity for devising new theories of the world. Even as a boy he had a toolmaker's chest in his room, which no one was allowed to touch. I was three or four years old then, and remember watching him for hours as he worked at his desk.

"How would you navigate?"

"The *Passarola* has sails."

"I mean how would you change altitude?"

"I can rise by means of a vacuum pump which exhausts air from the spheres and descend by injecting air into the spheres. There's also a ballast which I can drop to gain more height."

He tapped his fingers together and raised his eyebrows. "Anything else?"

A dim thought began to form in my mind. I might not win glory fighting Hottentots or sailing to India, but here was an opportunity to embark on an adventure that would attract the King's attention. I imagined soaring over deserts and volcanoes, jungles and oceans, drawing maps, rescuing the populations of besieged towns and exploring the farthest corners of the globe; and, I thought, my heroism would be something that Maria would approve of; and then, perhaps, she would pledge herself to me. ❦

# { 4 }

DAY AFTER day, week after week and piece by piece, we built the ship. Our patron, the Duke of Aveiro, allowed us the use of the empty granary on his estate. The building was concealed from his residence by trees and the path that led to it had become overgrown with brambles. It provided us with the perfect hideaway. Here we built a dry dock and laid the keel of the ship. I came to love the sound of the hammer, drumming out its tap, tap, tap, and the soft scraping noise of the saw cutting through fresh planks of timber. Even now, the smell of a carpenter's attic can send my mind racing back to those days when the air smelled of freshly planed wood and tar. We worked from early morning until midnight and awoke the next morning without feeling tired. We were young then. The heat did not sap us. Simple meals of bread, grilled sardines and olives were like manna and the water never tasted so pure and fresh as it did then.

The Duke paid us occasional visits and brought us news of the outside world. He was kind to us. A distant cousin on our mother's side, he often in-quired after her health—really wanting to know, I think, whether she was happy so far from home. His visits always caused me a great deal of excitement because I knew that if he was there then his favorite niece could not be far away. The real thrill for me was when Maria wandered down through the olive trees alone. She used to sit in a corner, patting Sacha or quietly reading a book. She was an aristocrat, of course, and watched us with the same impassive gaze that she must have reserved for her servants and lackeys. But sometimes, she would catch my eye and come over with the look of an eager pupil. "What is this-or-that?" she would ask, or "How does such-and-such a thing work?"

She could not understand why anyone would want to fly. How could I fail to see that the enter-prise was full of dangers? I used to flush at these re-marks and could barely control the tremor in my voice as I answered her questions. I wish that I had simply taken her inside the empty hull and held her in my arms, telling her that I wanted to fly because I loved her.

We built the ship in great secrecy for we feared that the Cardinal would use every possible means to prevent us from flying if he discovered our plans. The Duke was, of course, an accomplice and we had let Maria into our secret but nobody else at the court knew what we were up to. All our workmen were sworn to silence. The materials were purchased through intermediaries, who used false names, and we maintained several warehouses, moving about them only after dark.

From mahogany, we fashioned the ribs that supported the hull and from teak we constructed the hull itself. The sailcloth came from Genoa and the rigging from Spain. We found that the copper spheres had to be perfectly shaped because any imperfection caused them to crumple when evacuated. The only craftsmen who could deliver us the perfect specimen were Ottoman coppersmiths from Trabzon.

There were times, I admit, when I thought that the enterprise was futile and the sooner we cured ourselves of this foolish fancy the better. But my brother persevered. The silent spectacle of watching him at work with his long, slender fingers holding every kind of imaginable tool with casual confidence put me under the same spell that had captivated me as a child. All of his thoughts were fanatically fixed on the ship and, sure enough, we began to have our successes.

We connected the vacuum pump to the spheres and the apparatus rose, proving the Archimedean principle that lighter bodies floated in heavier fluids. Of course, we had our problems as well. The first few ascents were not very high as the ship tended to float at a height of a few hundred feet—a little more at dawn when the air was cooler—but rose no more. To make her lighter, we removed one of the masts and shortened the other so that the final design only had a single sail and a jib mast. A second sail at her rear, taut and smaller than the mainsail, served as the rudder; on it we painted the coat of arms of Portugal. It took us over a year but at last the *Passarola* was ready to be launched. &

# { 5 }

THOSE EARLY weeks following our maiden flight from São Jorge Castle seem endless now. It felt like we had discovered a new ocean—the sky, and its entire expanse lay out there for us to explore—all for ourselves. We braved air currents, we plowed into rainbows and we sailed through clouds. I have since read that in Saracen lands, the alchemists descend into the sea in glass spheres to observe the schools of fish and coral and the shafts of sunlight passing through the layers of water. I imagine that those voyagers must feel the same sense of wonder that we did; however, instead of schools of fish, we passed through clouds of butter-flies and flocks of migrating birds so thick that the entire world seemed sometimes filled with the flap-

27

ping of wings. The sky changed its colors too, becoming more diffuse as we climbed higher, just as the ocean becomes cooler at greater depths, the sky became cooler at greater heights. In fact, I sometimes had the impression that we human beings were creatures at the bottom of an ocean—creatures who could barely see the surface of this ocean that we called the "atmosphere"—and, like the fish that swim in our oceans, we had no comprehension of the world that lay beyond ours.

We flew to visit our mother's family in Porto and Lagos, carrying cakes and letters back and forth and exchanging bits of news among relatives who had not seen one another for years. We sailed over mountains where no one had marked the terrain. We familiarized ourselves with the compass. Then we sailed out over the open sea. Five or ten miles offshore we loosened the reefs and sailed downwind. We sailed in hard gales and heavy showers. We sailed at night. We learned to measure latitude by the stars. And for our final rite of passage, we journeyed to the Azores.

The eight-hundred-mile journey took us three days. We sighted some fishing boats a few leagues from the coast; the next day we saw the mastheads of a Spanish convoy. We passed them all without being sighted. In latitude 38° 20' north, we were hindered by a strong and contrary wind and found great difficulty in keeping our course. The sea ran high and thunder rolled over our heads. The *Passarola* bobbled on the currents like a cork bobbles on waves. The sail luffed around the mast and the boom slammed across the deck like a baton. Several times the simple maneuver of tacking windward nearly threw me overboard but for all the weariness, it was a joyous time. I felt the same excitement as a child sitting in a tree while the branches rustle and lightning tears through the clouds. We traveled for five or six hours in this weather until the sky darkened and the rain was pouring over the deck in torrents. Tired and drenched, we jammed the rudder and trimmed the sails to let the ship fly downwind. Then we closed the hatches behind us and went below deck.

This little space was our refuge. A ladder from the deck led into a small room that we used as the armory and wardrobe. Here we left our wet oilskins and proceeded down a narrow passage amidships, some ten feet long, which opened into a tiny galley at the rear of the ship. It was a cramped passage, and one had to duck chunks of dried meat, bread, sausages and damp undergarments dangling from hooks above. The galley had a small coal-fired stove. We lit it but it gave out a great deal of smoke so we ate our meal cold. Then we lit a charcoal burner for warmth and took turns to sleep. I rested till midnight while Bartolomeu went up to steer the ship and then I took my turn at the helm while he slept.

Our cabins were tucked away in the forecastle. Each had a small round window, one on the starboard and the other on the port side. Bartolomeu's cabin was slightly roomier than mine, although lockers for storing provisions took up most of the extra space. It also had a spare table and chair, bolted to the floor, which we used sometimes for eating our meals. With his book-lined shelves and pictures on the wall, his cabin actually had quite a cosy aspect. My own cabin was a cell with only enough room for a cot. It measured eight feet long by six feet wide with two perpendicular walls, and the third wall curved, being the inside of the hull itself. When I went to sleep that night, I could hear the muffled drumming of raindrops on the deck.

The next morning was fine and sunny. The sky was blue and bare without the shred of a cloud and the horizon was open wide. I stood in the crisp air, enjoying the sun on my face when I saw the outline of São Miguel rise into view. The black crest of an old volcanic cone cascaded down in steps of successive gradients to green meadows, blue hydrangea hedgerows and brown sands. This sight excited in me an emotion of delight unlike any I had ever felt. Cold and damp, I thought of the pleasures of my sedentary life—the fireside, the warm meals, the company of friends. All those things seemed insipid compared to the spectacle of this arcadia rising out of the taut blue sea.

Bartolomeu came and stood beside me.

"Sublime, is it not?" he remarked. "To find oneself balanced between the heaven and the abyss. True ecstasy is found there. There is the stillness and solitude that drives off the spleen, but lightning bolts dangle over our heads and storms brew in those clouds. A compelling experience it is, to be sure."

I nodded. I would not have traded places with a king. ℮

# { 6 }

I T WAS not very long after our flight to the
Azores that His Majesty invited us to the Casa da
India for a royal dinner. The reception was held in
the grand saloon, where shafts of the last remaining
sunlight shone through its tall narrow windows
and set ablaze the great crystal chandeliers that
hung from the frescoed ceiling. In the midst of the
saloon a table was laid out for a hundred guests. No-
bles, diplomats, foreign kings, rajas and dignitaries
moved down its length to their seats, murmuring
greetings to one another and making polite conversation. Finally came the King and Queen, followed
by the train of the Cardinal and his bishops and
archbishops. I could never tell which assembly was

greater—the arrival of His Majesty and his Queen or the entrance of the Pope's vassals, but as the royals entered, I do recall that several hundred guests rose in unison with one sound of rustling silk.

I sat toward one end of the Cardinal's table. Maria Veldavez and her uncle sat opposite my brother and me, with the Cardinal seated at the table head. Gold-plated silverware adorned the table and red candles flickered in candlesticks of pure gold. At a sign from the master of ceremonies, the line of valets standing against the wall moved as one, like automata, and began to bring out the dishes—stuffed fowl served on glazed white Meissen porcelain, and carp, truffled quails, mutton with garlic and a roast pheasant, all served with fresh asparagus and early green peas.

It was a splendid evening. Maria was a little aloof as we sat down for dinner but after many glasses of cherry brandy, she and I were exchanging bold glances and smiling as we overheard the conversation elsewhere. I listened to the Cardinal's words above the others.

"It is a wonder," he said, glancing around the table, "that the copper spheres lift a body as large as the *Passarola*, yet I am convinced that it will not transgress the heavens. I see problems ahead."

The remark was intended to smite my brother and its effect was immediate.

"Why?" Bartolomeu snapped.

The old inquisitor smiled thinly. "For the spheres create a void and it is a known fact that nature abhors a void. It is the greatest evil and any experiment that re-creates it is unnatural and heretical."

My brother shook his head. "Saint Augustine himself has affirmed that God created the world from a void, *ex nihilo*, through a free act of His will. If all creation arose from a void then how could such a thing be unnatural?"

"Because God has done away with the void," the Cardinal replied. "Is it not Descartes who says that the universe is full of corporeal matter and the void between the planets is not a vacuum but an ether, which is a plenum in which the planets revolve around the sun, like leaves in a vortex of water?"

The Duke of Aveiro put down his knife and fork. "Your Excellency!" he said. "Would you object if flying machines rose on the principle of hot air?"

"I have an objection if things are on the wrong

34

path," the Cardinal replied civilly but with eyes ablaze. "Flying machines are evil because they will bring great disturbance to mankind. Those who possess them will use them against those without. No city and no state will be proof against their consequences."

"They will also bring good," my brother remarked.

"Do you not see? All those who tried to fly have fallen to their deaths."

"Or been tried by the Inquisition. I do see!"

"God will not permit it."

"But whatever exists in men's minds is part of a divine plan, and because men have conceived flying machines, therefore these machines must be part of the divine plan, *cito fit quod deii volunt*."

"Perhaps," the Cardinal said coolly, "but you forget that the designs of the Evil One also appear in many guises."

"Then we must ensure to foil his designs," Bartolomeu replied. "I will arrange to send the *Passarola* to our Pope. He could use it to visit his vassals around the world and cut evil at its root."

"Father! God holds us accountable for our work," the Cardinal cried. "What you are doing is sorcery.

You are opposing the will of God by breaking natural laws. Confess and repent in this world for you are committing a sin."

"Confess? And what's the price? Will you burn me at the stake?"

Tobacco smoke hung thick in the air. I inhaled its aroma and felt light-headed. I saw the Duke shaking his head. I saw the Cardinal frowning. I watched as my brother kissed the Cardinal's episcopal ring and left the table. But I was strangely oblivious to the entire exchange. The chatter of people was becoming a monotonous din. My thoughts wandered, my head swam and in the reflection of gilt wood mirrors, I saw the reflection of Maria's eyes. I felt the gentle knock of someone's foot against my leg, and my first thought was that it was Maria's. She was leaning toward me to be heard. She was asking about our voyage to the Azores. Never had I bathed in the splendor of my own narration as I did that night. I told her about the perils I had faced in the Atlantic—the sixty-knot winds, the foaming rollers, the whales and the many albatrosses that we had encountered had all existed for this moment alone.

She leant toward me again. "How high can you fly?"

"So high that the mountains seem like anthills."

"Higher than the birds?"

"Oh, we go much higher than the birds," I replied. "The birds catch our droppings."

She giggled. "If you fly so high, won't you get burnt by the sun?"

"That's possible," I said. I explained that the *Passarola* could sail past the sun and all the other planets in the same way as a girl pirouettes from the arms of one gentleman to another. With that swashbuckling remark, I stood, and was about to ask her for a dance when she motioned me to sit back down again.

"Where would you go?" she asked.

"To the end of the universe."

She settled her hazel eyes upon me. "What for?"

Her fragrance, her pearly teeth, her loosely gathered curls intoxicated me. The cherry brandy coursed through my veins. My cheeks felt hot. "For you," I said.

"You are a brave man."

My courage grew. "I would like to take you for an excursion," I said.

"It's late."

"It's never late."

Her eyes shone. "You want to go at this hour?"

"Precisely."

"But what of your brother?"

I looked around the room and spotted him surrounded by some French *philosophes*.

"One day we would all be living in great flying machines as vast as cities, all suspended from gigantic vacuum spheres," I heard him saying. "We will abandon the earth and take to the sky."

"But, monsieur, why leave the earth at all?" one of the gentlemen asked.

"Because the earth is finite; it has borders. The sky is infinite and without borders; men will live in it in freedom."

"Man creates borders wherever he goes," another person whom I recognized to be Voltaire replied. "Man wishes to sleep on this side of the bed and his wife on that but trouble comes when they both wish to sleep on the same side."

At this remark, the gentlemen laughed most heartily. "But I digress," Voltaire continued, finger pointing skyward. "What I wished to say was why we create borders; does anyone know? Because we are bound by our thoughts."

"Are you challenging Reason?" A short man blustered. He had stretched himself to his full height. "I must ask you at once. You, sir—the same man who once championed Reason now questions it. Do you have any convictions at all?"

Voltaire was pulling at the locks of his wig, an infamous habit, which meant that he was preparing for a long argument. "You are right," he said, bowing deeply. "I quite forgot that I did champion it. Well, squire, here is another demonstration of how a perfectly reasonable man falls victim to the frailty of being human. But since you challenge my convictions, I must say that I do not hold on to them tightly. When their time passes, I let them go."

I could see that the discussion would continue into the night. My heart was beating fast. I had no doubt that in that time, I could bring the *Passarola* safely back without Bartolomeu's even finding out that anything was amiss.

"My brother can talk all night," I said to Maria. "What about your uncle?"

"Him?" She glanced over my shoulder. "He's at a game of cards. If he wins, he won't leave the table until dawn. If he loses, he'll play till noon."

"Then it's settled?"

She straightened her gloves and giving me a final

39

glance, left the table surreptitiously. A moment later, I rose and followed her. We made our way out of the throng and came to the portico where the carriages waited. Our coats were brought up. Two white steeds pulled a lacquered black carriage up the cobblestones. The coachman, an old soldier with a waxed moustache and a drooping eyelid, rose from his seat, creaking with the inertia of old bones, to open the door for Maria. But before he could get to it, I had opened it already and in a flurry of crino-line and velvet, had tumbled in beside her. ℰ

## { 7 }

THE *Passarola* ideally needed two men to steer the ship; one person manned the boom and the other the tiller but in my supreme confidence— I could have circumnavigated the globe in that drunken state—I decided to ride it solo. I lowered the gangway for Maria and followed her aboard. I rolled up the sails and untied the mooring. The pump made a whooshing sound as the copper spheres were evacuated. And gently, like a leaf rising on a current of warm air, the *Passarola* rose. Maria leant over the gunnel and watched the landscape recede below her. It was a dark night but glittered with lamps and lanterns here and there. Maria undid the ribbons in her hair and let the locks fall.

"Oh, it's so quiet!" she murmured.

"We don't hear the wind because we travel with it."

"But it's so cold," she said, twisting her gloves.

I felt a thrill and drew her close to me. Her tone became softer. "Sometimes," she said, almost whispering, "when I sit alone on the roof on warm nights, I see a star moving in the night sky and wonder if it's you."

"That would be a shooting star," I replied, smiling.

Maria sighed and made a soft sound. "But then, I was only being metaphorical," she said. "I am a fanciful creature. Did you know what I dreamt the other night? I dreamt that we were traveling together in the *Passarola*—the two of us, yes ... visiting the great courts of Europe. It was wonderful, so wonderful! But then I awoke and realized that you had left me. A gust of wind had filled your sails and carried you away."

I looked at her. Her face was a few inches from mine. I could smell the faint whiff of liquor on her breath.

"Tell me, sir," she continued, clasping my arm gently, "when you sleep in your cabin at night, sailing alone above the earth, what do you dream?"

I looked at the dark mass of the sea a thousand

feet below. I wanted to say that I dreamt of her but the words that escaped my lips were, "I dream to see all the countries and all the people of the world."

She raised her eyes. "Then what you said to me at dinner, that couldn't have been too deep."

I began to protest but she smiled insouciantly and put her finger on my lips.

"I hope you won't fall in love with me," she said.

"But I *am* in love with you."

She gave me a long glance. "You are a sweet creature. I will only make you suffer. I will bring you nothing but misery. Oh, it is in my nature! I scorn the lips that kiss me. I spite the men who love me. I am a cruel woman."

I was thrown into the deepest confusion. The girl who, a moment ago, seemed such a vulnerable creature now appeared to me in the guise of a terrible coquette. But I knew then as I know now that it was too late. I had already surrendered myself to her wiles and her admission, her dire warning, only added to her charms so that I was urged further to take the risk.

"One could get tired of wandering," she suddenly said.

"One could get tired staying in one place."

"Not if you're happy."

"Are you?"

She gave a sigh. "I don't know," she said.

As I held her, she clung to me tightly and pressed her lips to mine. A strong breeze carried us along. The sails fluttered in the wind and our ship plunged headlong into thick cloud. Hail, the size of pebbles, pelted against the deck. Everything on board—the sails, our clothes, the deck itself—became cold and wet. Storm clouds gathered around us and in the distance, we heard thunder. Then the rain came rolling in sheets. Lightning bolts cut through the sky. The wind was so strong that it threatened to blow us out to the sea. I kept throwing ballast overboard until the ship had climbed above the clouds. Then, holding her hand, I led her below deck and closed the hatch behind us. ℰ

## { 8 }

MARIA WAS my first love. I loved her with complete abandon, with blissful disregard of all portents. I knew that she did not love me back and I never believed that I could truly possess her; but this knowledge, instead of restraining me, turned my love into a heady passion. I close my eyes and the memory, as it comes back to me even today, gives me the rush of being an adolescent again. I was content and I felt a satisfaction with my life as I had never known. It was the sweetest thing for me to know that I had loved—yes, loved—a woman and I felt then as I have never felt again that even if I wasted my life away, even if I dropped dead the next instant, I would have no regrets because I had tasted love.

It was, of course, an illusion.

The spell broke a few days later. I arrived at the palace and discovered to my dismay that the courtiers were winking at me and various ladies at the court were rolling their eyes. *"Senhor,"* the women would say, "what must we do for a ride?" or "Can you show us the stars?" and titter at their own witticisms. One can imagine my horror at this exposé. A group of sentries had reported seeing the *Passarola* over the Casa da India on the night of the reception. They thought that it had been stolen and from this, the rumor spread that one of the brothers had enjoyed a mistress on board the ship. The mystery of her identity increased the scandal. I felt that it was only a matter of time before the coachman opened his mouth, or some other witness came forward and unraveled the truth.

I do not know how one thing led to another but I suppose that the Cardinal's men were at work. Hearsay and lies spread by his spies were added to the scandal and slowly, the Chinese whispers turned into a story where the Queen and my brother were substituted for Maria and me. The Queen was still without child, it was said, because she had been seduced by *O Voador*; she could not experience ecstasy with the King any more unless the simulation of flying was re-created—a thunderstorm raged outside, rain pelted on the windows and a party of Hottentot slaves shook the royal bed.

Everyone knew that the scandal had no basis but the King was not amused. Bartolomeu was pronounced guilty of dragging the Queen's name in mud and stripped of all his royal privileges. The sentence, although the lightest possible, disturbed us greatly. The Cardinal had sat through the interrogation caressing his ring with eyes half closed, a victorious smile on his face. This was a bad omen. Now that we were out of royal favor, he was free to do with us what he pleased.

As for Maria, the night we spent together was our first and last. Although I never let slip any boasts, she blamed me for the gossip and said that I had ruined her. I begged her for an audience but she stopped coming to the court. I went to her residence but I was told that she had gone away. No one knew where and when she would return. I wrote her letters, each more desperate than the other, proclaiming my innocence and hoping that someone would pass them on to her. When she did not reply, I fell into the blackest despair. I loitered at operas and outside theaters in the forlorn hope of falling at her feet and pleading to her for forgiveness. She did not come. The weeks that followed have left no impression on my mind. It was as if I were outside myself, going through the motions of living without having my heart in it. I have no other memory of that period except a sense of fruitlessness. Oh, how I suffered! It never occurred to me that perhaps she had amused herself with me and her thirst quenched, chose not to reply; that perhaps our romance was not meant to be. Instead the more neglected I felt, the more I wanted to possess her. When a friend brought me word that Maria had another suitor, the news struck me to the heart. I sank into a state of complete dejection and would have willingly flung myself at my rival with a pair of pistols.

Bartolomeu did not rebuke me, though I was the cause of our trouble. He was always in high spirits from his ascents and tried to divert my attention by taking me up on his flights.

"Almost all women here have lovers," he told me. "Sometimes they have more than one. If you become their lover then you must play by their game. It all means nothing to them. They'll have a new one tomorrow. They have such free manners."

I could not bring myself to believe this. "How do you know?" I remarked bitterly. "Have you ever been in love?"

"I have resolved not to fall in love," he said. "Don't mistake me—love is a great and terrible passion but if one must have a vocation, then it is a distraction. One must make sacrifices if one is to achieve any-thing in this world. I have no time for distractions. For my vocation, I have sacrificed love."

"Then you are immune from all suffering," I re-marked.

"Oh, I suffer a great deal more than you think," he chuckled. "I suffer because I deny myself what others have. My discipline causes me to suffer. Do you think I do not miss the rustle of feminine dresses? The laughter, the scent of cologne on pretty companions? Do you think that I do not yearn to be with the parties that ride to picnics in their carriages? I do, so much. But I have tasted the silence of the heavens, and despite myself, and de-spite the rush and bustle of life that I desire, I pre-fer its stillness."

To be sure, flying brought my heart into my mouth and made me forget my sorrow, but there was also another attraction to it: my conscience was burdened by a sense of guilt. I felt that I had done him wrong. He had been disgraced on my account and his life was now in danger. I felt that I needed to redeem myself somehow. I would serve my time by following him, I thought, like a novice follows a monk. I would embrace the severities of aerial life like those Christians who practiced self-flagellation as a penance for their sins. With this resolve and the hope that time would prove an amnesiac, I threw myself with gusto into my brother's flights. ℰ

# { 9 }

SEVERAL WEEKS passed without incident. Meanwhile, the Cardinal became unduly courteous and polite and did his best to befriend Bartolomeu. We knew, of course, that he was playing a game; he was doing everything possible to keep his prey in sight while setting a trap to snare him. I am not going to relate what precautions we took but to say that they were thorough. We armed ourselves with guns and stockpiled a cache of powder at the granary large enough to blow the entire neighborhood into the sky. Then one afternoon, the Cardinal sent his men. My brother and I were resting in the servant's quarters behind the granary. A soft sea breeze was blowing through the olive trees. Bartolomeu was smoking his pipe and I was lying on a settee. The gentle sound of leaves rustling and the cooing of doves had lulled me to sleep when I was startled by the thud of heavy steps climbing the stairs. Swords clanked outside our door and there was a rude knock.

"Is *O Voador* there?" a deep voice thundered.

"Who cares to know?" I shouted back.

"The Holy Office of the Inquisition," the voice replied.

Bartolomeu put out his pipe and stood up.

"Why?" I asked.

"'Why?' he asks!" Laughter followed. "*O Voador* is under arrest," the voice shouted. "He must surrender himself."

"Charges?"

"Sorcery."

The door rattled. Bartolomeu shook his head. "This is the end," he said. He lifted a musket out of its rack and started toward the door.

I leapt at him and held him by his arm.

"Wait! What are you doing?"

"The Cardinal wants my scalp," he said as he primed the charge. "He shall have it but not without a fight."

I tightened my grip. I told him that I was determined to fight with him, but I had no intention of losing my life. "The *Passarola* is tethered outside," I said. "If we are lively, we can still make our escape and return to throw firebombs at our accusers."

"His Holiness will not be delayed," the voice shouted. "Open the door!"

The soldiers pushed against the door. We had bolted it from inside but now we dragged a tall cabinet from across the room and piled a table behind that. When it looked like the barricade would hold for a while, we quickly gathered all the guns and powder that we could carry. We were looking around in a great hurry to see if there was anything else we could salvage when Bartolomeu suddenly stopped and said, "Where's Sacha?"

My arms were full of weapons and my heart beat fast. I looked around the small room with some annoyance. The dog had suddenly vanished. We heard a faint bark in the distance but we could not wait. Bartolomeu shook his head and I nodded.

"Let's go," I said.

We left through the back door and ran up the stairwell to the roof, where the *Passarola* was moored. As we threw our guns on board, we heard the soldiers crashing through our barricade below.

53

The first shots rang out in the stairwell as we scrambled aboard. I lashed out at the moorings with my knife. My brother clapped my shoulder.

"Hurry!" he shouted. "How many are there against us?"

One by one, the grenadiers emerged from the stairwell. I made a quick reckoning and counted a dozen.

"Twelve," I said, "Maybe more."

The thick rope finally ripped but no sooner had we pushed the *Passarola* away from its post than we saw the soldiers aiming their guns at the vacuum spheres. Bartolomeu had already primed his pistols and was firing with guns in both hands. The ship's deck was thick with smoke. Musket balls were smashing into the hull and shards of timber were flying in the air. I ducked under the bulwarks and primed my own double-barreled pistol. I had never harmed a man before, let alone killed one, but I knew that if I did not kill them first, they would kill me. This rudimentary fact swept away every other emotion. So I stood up and fired into the throng below.

"Save yourselves if you can!" I cried, as three or four grenadiers fell in my first discharge.

A swarm of musket balls buzzed past my head.

The vacuum pump was draining the spheres and the *Passarola* was rising, but with horrible sluggishness. I crouched low as I hoisted the mainsail and low-ered the jib to catch wind. Bartolomeu was throw-ing lines, anchor and ballast across the side.

"Helm to port!" he shouted above the din. "To-ward the sea. Quick!"

A weak breeze filled our sails and gently tugged our ship out toward the harbor. Soon we had sailed over half the city. The ship's shadow was slipping and sliding over houses, gardens and public squares. Some of the soldiers pursued us on the ground but they gave up one by one and by the time we reached the harbor, none of our foes were in sight. But the saddest sight was of Sacha. The poor dog chased us through the winding lanes until he lost his way in some blind alley. His barks became fainter and fainter until we heard him no more.

The departure weighed heavily on my heart. Everything had happened so quickly that only af-terward did I find myself troubled by a great many doubts. I worried about Maria. I worried what my parents might think of the situation Bartolomeu and I had found ourselves in. I worried about our own fates. What we ought to do, where we ought to

55

go, and whether we ought not to return and face our accusers like men. These were the thoughts that passed through my mind.

"We'd better say our good-bye to Portugal now," Bartolomeu said when he saw me brooding, "for there's no coming back here, that's to be sure."

"Why, the King would revoke the charges if he would hear our tale. We have done no wrong."

"No wrong? Half a dozen soldiers lie in their blood back there and you say that we have done no wrong. Those are soldiers of the Inquisition that we have killed, Alex. We'll be tried by a court with Conti presiding and half a dozen cardinals in the jury. What will the King do? Do you think he will challenge their verdict? He won't dare. Where there's no justice, there won't be any clemency."

"What should we do now?" I asked, whereupon he became very grave and said that we had to flee from here. Our only hope of asylum lay in France. Madrid would almost certainly cooperate in our hunt, he thought; there was no refuge to be found there. So we had two options: we could sail north-east, cross the Tagus and make our way across the Spanish border to Valladolid and from there to Pamplona and then across the French border to Gascogne.

At a little over five hundred miles, depending on winds, the route was the shortest, but it ran the gauntlet across the plateau where we could be easily followed by horsemen. The other option was to circumvent the peninsula entirely. We could head south to the Gulf of Cadiz, turn east to cross the Strait of Gibraltar and hug the coastline along the Mediterranean, passing the Costa del Sol, crossing the thirty-eighth parallel up north to Costa Blanca, pass Valencia and Barcelona and then make a dash to Perpignan. This tortuous path was twice as long as the land route but it allowed us the relative safety of the open sea. Storms and squalls on one hand and the hand of the Inquisition on the other. It was a dubious choice. ৫

# { 10 }

WE HAD drifted out into the open sea when the wind carried to us the faint sound of shanties. Presently, a galleon sailed into view. Bartolomeu looked at it through his telescope and then passed the glasses to me.

"Take a look!"

It was a three-masted ship flying the Portuguese colors. The men on board were singing in hoarse baritones, heaving up the sails on the beat. I could make out an ensign perched in the crow's nest, peering up at us through his telescope. Our sights crossed and for a moment, the ensign and I stared at each other from afar through our lenses.

"Alex, turn three points to port," Bartolomeu said, "let's see what she does."

"Aye, brother," I replied and with my heart racing, set about making sail. I had a disturbing feeling that we were being hunted and sure enough, as we turned windward, the galleon loosened her sails and turned also.

"Now, turn three points to starboard."

I trimmed the sails. The *Passarola* turned and as we expected, the galleon's bow followed. No sooner did we see her turn than our minds were made up. We would head back to the shore and travel inland. I tried to come about and sail with the wind but it was not blowing constantly in force or even in the same direction and the *Passarola* began to shake so violently that I thought it would fall. The sails luffed around the mast and at times they filled out. The canvas thundered in my ears. The ship trembled in the currents. When the sails were useful again, we beat windward at great speed. The galleon fell behind. The sea changed its color from dull green to deep blue, the rollers flashed past and we were over the coast.

We began following a dirt road heading north and dropped a log line to mark our speed. Soon we spotted a small band of cavalry in pursuit of us. The light breeze pushed the *Passarola* along at twenty or thirty knots and the cavalry had no trouble closing the gap. They shot our log to pieces and tried to pull us down by tugging at the line that dragged behind the ship. Soon they were galloping right below us, yelling and firing their guns up into the air. We shook them off by leaving the dirt road and flying over a terrain of farmland and rolling hills. The next time I peered through my telescope, the posse was skirting around some bogs. Soon they were as small as beetles and when I looked again, they had disappeared from sight entirely.

We were some four hours in the air and about eighty miles from Lisbon. A strong northwesterly current was pushing us along. The air grew cold over the highlands and our ship, becoming lighter, gained more height. The barometer indicated three thousand feet. The ship furrowed through scattered balls of cumulus clouds, which made us damp and cold. We could see the curvature of the earth at this elevation. The horizon was yellow with the glow of twilight, but the splendor of our surroundings was of little concern to us because we had to be on our feet, coiling ropes, hoisting the sails, and taking turns piloting the vessel.

Soon after midnight, Bartolomeu retired for

some rest while I steered. The breeze abated some-what, so I jammed the tiller and sat back against the bulwarks. My clothes were wet but I had noth-ing else to wear. I lit my pipe and puffed into my hands to keep them warm. The air was clear and the stars shone with a remarkable brilliance. The sky was littered with galaxies that glowed as if they had been washed in phosphorus. Comets tore through the void, burning bright like fireflies be-fore vanishing into the inky blue. Now that the discomfort and cares of those earlier hours have paled, my only recollection is that it was a beauti-ful night.

§

TOWARD THREE o'clock in the morning, we changed watch. I lay in my cot with my eyes shut but I was aware of every sound, thinking at every moment that the ship would meet some disaster. It is the same when a man bivouacs for the first time in the wilderness. A leaf rustles and his heart misses a beat. A hare jumps through the undergrowth and he wakes with a start. Each time there was a noise, my eyes flew open to learn the source. Each time the ship rolled, I winced with dread. I twisted and turned under my fur skins and barely slept—it was a fitful stupor.

In the morning, I awoke with an aching body. It was a cloudless day. The sun shone in my face through the porthole. Hoarfrost covered the sails and in the bright light, the canvas sparkled white. A cuckoo cooed somewhere. I looked over the gunnel and saw a wisp of smoke drifting upward. I took our bearings and found that we had traveled three degrees of latitude, which was nearly three hundred miles over the last fourteen hours. It was a fair accomplishment and with the wind prevailing, we estimated arriving at Valladolid by late afternoon.

A farmhouse appeared in the distance. We watched the thin trail of smoke rise from its chimney. The sight of an orchard next to the property awakened my hunger.

"Why bless my soul, Alex," Bartolomeu said. "Would they break their bread with us, you think?"

The *Passarola* had not been primed for a long flight and we were without provisions. We had hung a canvas above the deck overnight to collect moisture from the air but there was barely a cupful of liquid in it. In fact, the few drops of dew that it collected during the night were frozen in the morning. After making certain that there was no one in sight, we loosened the valves on the spheres and made our way toward the orchard. By degrees, the *Passarola* descended until its hull was scraping the treetops. I leant over the bulwarks and plucked an apple from a branch; next, some oranges; and then, as Bartolomeu brought the craft around, I swept over the apple trees again. Soon the deck was rolling in fruit. Encouraged by our success, we decided to pluck some chickens from a coop nearby or perhaps even a whole sheep and leave behind some coins in exchange.

A large sheepdog suddenly appeared below us, barking furiously. Two small boys with dirty faces came running after it a moment later and following the animal's gaze, looked up at the *Passarola*. I thought that they would take us for some infernal machine and bolt but, instead, they started pelting us with stones. When the stones hit the hull with a thunk, their courage rose and they threw another volley—harder this time. The older boy finally mustered the nerve to speak.

"You! What are you doing up there?" he shouted.

Bartolomeu doffed his tricorne. *"¡Señor!"* he replied. "Would you congratulate your father for keeping a

63

bountiful orchard. It looks particularly ripe from up here."

Seeing that we were no demons, the boy became furious. He flung a missile at my brother. "You steal my fruit, you thief! I'll kill you!"

Bartolomeu ducked. "I can return your fruit from here," he offered.

"*¡Que se vaya a la mierda!*"

"Would you like to do a barter with us?" I retorted.

The boy's eyes grew large. "*¿Por favor?*"

"We are on an adventure," I said. "We are hungry and we've not had anything to eat. If you let us have some of your fruit and other provisions from your farm then we'll show you our ship. Have you ever seen a ship like this? *Una aeronave . . .* "

"*No, señor.*"

"Well, would you want to see it?"

This offer proved irresistible to the little rascals. They nodded at each other and in an instant, dropped their missiles. We told them to bring us a chicken, some onions, pepper, tomatoes and fire-wood and they were obedient and lively with the summons. We lowered the rope ladder and allowed them to remain on board for some time. They wandered about the deck with furtive steps for a little

64

while—as if afraid that they might step on or touch something which would send the ship to the ground—but when they observed that the *Passarola* held steady, curiosity overcame their fear. They invented a jumping game to rock the ship and chased each other up and down the deck. After their games grew a little tired, we pressed a silver piece each in their palms and returned them to the ground and their barking dog. ℰ

# { 11 }

WE SAILED east and allowed a fair distance between ourselves and the farm before we turned north. The sun shone brightly and reflected its light upon the Tagus, a silver thread that ran a few miles away on our starboard. We made landfall on a deserted bank and soon had a roaring bonfire going. We made a fine meal of it all—saying grace beforehand—and washed it down with a bottle of sherry that my brother conjured from the ship's hold. One would have thought that the circumstances of our escape might have cooled my passion for flying, but the savage joy of eating and sleeping under the open sky was like a tonic. It seemed to me then the best way to spend one's life.

"Why are you smiling, Alex?" my brother asked. "What's the matter?"

"I feel happy," I said.

"Oh? You're not sad about leaving?"

I was a little melancholy of course, but what could I say? The sky had set us free and by degrees, I realized the magnitude of this freedom. We could cross boundaries and fences and go where we pleased. No sovereign had power here, except ourselves, and the world lay at our feet. I had never felt a more ardent desire to be an aeronaut.

After we had smoked our pipes, we continued our journey. It was a beautiful afternoon. Beams of golden sunlight streaked through the dusty white clouds. The shadows of almond trees fell long across bales of hay. As we sailed over red-roofed farmhouses and fields of bright yellow sunflowers, I quite forgot myself and merrily doffed my tricorne at the peasant women below. They crossed themselves and screamed, *"¡Madre mía!"* as they fled. This play amused me for a while but my brother unfurled the sails to hasten our progress. We were flying low. The ship had become sluggish and heavy in the warm air but her sails were soon full again and the breeze grew strong, and so, quite content with our circumstances, we let her run downwind to Valladolid.

As we arrived over the township, children chased us across the squares, women looked out of their windows and men stood at street corners, pointing at our ship and gesticulating wildly. When we greeted them with shouts of *"¡Señoras y señores! ¡Buenos días!"* and waved and bowed from our ship, a procession began to follow us—the youths running and skipping along and the others riding horses.

*"¿De donde?"* they shouted. *"Marte Vallis? Luna?"*

*"¡Portugal!"* we shouted back, to which there were cries of astonishment.

*"¿Usted viene en paz?"*

*"Sí, señor, somos amigos."*

We even saw some gilded carriages gliding through the throng and the odd lame fellow hopping madly behind the rest. The procession grew larger and larger until there were hundreds of people following in our wake. Since they had to navigate their way through the town, while we flew unhindered, I can only describe their progress like a snake slithering through a labyrinth—slow around corners, fast along straight paths, stretching out on curves and compact while passing through squares.

The cathedral lay in our path. Its ramparts loomed ahead and we could see they swarmed with people. But as we drew closer, we realized that these people were not well-wishers but cuirassiers. Their breastplates glinted in the sun and they were armed to the teeth. For a few precious moments, we did not know whether they were friendly or hostile and when we perceived that they were raising their weapons, we hastened to prime our own guns; but by then it was too late. The first shot tore through the mainsail. The second shot ripped through the hull of the ship and some wood splinters hit me in the face. Then followed a volley of shots that blew our mainsail to bits. The rudder was also peppered with balls and the integrity of our spheres was in jeopardy. Bartolomeu prepared to yank at the jib but the fabric tore in the wind and completely crippled our ship. I loaded my pistol and fired at the soldiers. They replied with long guns and carbines. The air below us was rent with white puffs and the smell of cordite. I thought that we were done for this time, but then I realized that many of the shots were falling out of range. A gust of hot air blowing in from the land had filled our sails and was slowly pulling the ship upward. All at once, there was an explosion beneath my feet and the floor tore up, sending shards of timber flying into the air. I was blinded by the blast. I fired once. The report of the pistol rang in my ear and I fell.

When I opened my eyes again, I was lying in my cot. Bright sunlight streamed in from the porthole, but the air was noticeably cooler. I felt for the wound. The ball had grazed me above my left shoulder. It had broken through skin and touched some muscle but not badly. I was already feeling much better. Bartolomeu had thrown some rugs and silks to cover me but still I shivered from cold. I could hear a strong wind blowing outside, buffeting the ship as if it was a living thing struggling to free itself from the vise of a gigantic hand. I opened the scuttle to climb onto the deck but as soon as I raised the lid, the wind screamed in my ears.

"We're two miles above the ground!" cried Bartolomeu.

"How fast are we going?"

"What?"

"How fast?"

"Sixty knots."

We were sailing across the wind and this gave us a great sensation of speed. We turned to the rolling pastures north by northeast where vines and maize fields grew next to meadows of trefoil. Then we trimmed the sails and everything was quiet again. The land below flashed past like pictures from a magic lantern. We flew over hills and clumps of wild olives and figs. Townships came and went one after the other. It seemed to us that a current of air had lifted the *Passarola* from its low elevation and flung it miraculously thousands of feet up into the sky. Here a great river of wind flowed, deep and wide, which carried us along like driftwood.

§

WE CROSSED the land mass of Spain at great speed. When I look at my maps now, I can see that we cut 4° west of longitude the following morning and by noon, we had crossed the Paris meridian. In the afternoon, the breeze slackened and we drifted for several hours. Puffs of wind stirred our ship in one direction and then another. The sun was setting when the wind freshened to a twenty-knot easterly breeze. We were hungry and tired but grateful of

Providence, we turned north and sailed through the night.

At sunrise the next day, I saw Bartolomeu, his hands clasped behind his back, standing in the bow. When I joined him there, he pointed to something in the distance. On the horizon, I could make out the skyline of a great city in the morning fog. "Have we reached Gascogne?" I asked my brother but he did not know. The fog became thicker and thicker and almost seemed like a wall that hemmed us in on all sides when we plunged in it. We could not even see the bow from the stern. It was as if we were sailing through a gray plenum devoid of the sun and the horizon and lacking in all dimensions—for we could not tell whether we were ten feet above the ground or a hundred. We proceeded with great caution, at a speed of five knots or so, and breathed freely only when we saw the spire of Notre Dame looming above us. ℰ

# { 12 }

W E STAYED briefly at Saint-Germain-en-Laye with Voltaire, who maintained a safe house for all those who incurred the Vatican's wrath. It was a happy sojourn but our arrival in Paris had not gone unobserved. The sight of the airship moving low across the sky drew attention from miles away. We began to suspect that we were being watched and this feeling was vindicated one evening.

We were dining with Voltaire and his friends in the central hall. From the tall windows, we could see the twilight lingering over the trees, the darkening fields and the black mass of the forest, which rang with the howls of foxes. Our circle of candlelight seemed to us then to be the only radiance left in a world plunged in darkness. We were freethinkers and saw ourselves as the new champions of liberal ideas. Newton was our god and the gospel of Locke was on everyone's lips. We drank wine, spoke heresies and laughed at our wit. Everything seemed possible and there was so much hope.

I scarcely noticed the valet enter the room and glide past me, carrying a letter upon a silver tray for my brother. It was only after he had read the missive and his face grew dark that I became curious.

"Who delivered this letter?" he asked the lackey, who stood impassively against the wall.

"I believe it was a man, monsieur."

"My dear fellow," remarked Voltaire, who was a trifle gay after taking to the wine too freely, "did you perceive clearly and distinctly that it *was* a man? Are you sure that it was not something else, a demon perhaps?"

"I don't know, monsieur." The lackey's face was drained of all color. "My eyesight failed me in the gloom."

"What did he look like?" my brother asked.

"I could not see," the lackey said. "He wore a blue robe and a mask."

"Another Parisian reveler," one of the guests remarked, losing interest. "They are infamous for their tricks."

"Did he say anything?"

"No, sir."

"What mask did he wear?"

"It was a death's-head, monsieur."

There was a momentary silence in the room. I took the letter from Bartolomeu's hands and examined it. It was addressed to him and bore an invitation to a fancy-dress ball that was being held the next night at a house in the Place de Louis-le-Grand. There was nothing else to it, not even the sender's name.

"Most strange," Voltaire remarked, now as sober as I had ever seen him. "You must be careful, Father. There are half a dozen secret societies in Paris who want your machine and the agents of the Inquisition are, of course, never too far away. Shall I call upon the chief of police? I know him at the comissionary."

Bartolomeu shook his head and folded up the letter. "The writing is disguised and you have heard what your man had to say," he said. "We have no clues. I doubt if the authorities could throw any more light on this than us all gathered in this room."

"What do you intend to do?" I asked.

"Why, I intend to go," Bartolomeu said. "I will be surrounded by revelers and do not see any danger in it. If someone wishes to bring me to harm, he would not chose a ball for a rendezvous."

I hoped to help him clear up the mystery of this letter and so we decided to go to the ball together.

§

ON THE appointed night, we left the *Passarola* moored at Saint-Germain-en-Laye. After satisfying ourselves that our ship was properly guarded, we put on black dominos in the Venetian fashion and traveled to the house in a brougham.

As soon as we reached the neighborhood, we realized that we were being followed through the lanes by another carriage. At a street corner, we ordered our driver to stop and wait. Soon the other carriage passed. Its windows were drawn up but there was a pale yellow glow within and against the windowpane, we saw the fleeing image of a death's-head. This specter disappeared in the evening mist and by the time we arrived at the house, there was such gaiety and laughter that I put the episode out of my mind. We climbed up the marble steps of the grand staircase and crossed the ballroom, where countless dancers whirled. In a corner of the crush-room, we took our glasses of champagne and waited.

It was a sumptuous ball. I shall never forget it. All the windows and doors were festooned with gold ribbons. A large chandelier hung from the ceiling. Brocade chairs were arranged along the walls where pretty women ablaze with diamonds sat down to catch their breath between dancing quadrilles. The chamber was small itself but the mirrors on the walls and ceiling gave an illusion of a vast, infinite space filled with dancers and revelers.

Bartolomeu wore a half mask and a pair of large white wings on his robe. It was something that I had suggested he wear in jest. I wore a mask shaped like an eagle's beak but it was my brother who drew the stares.

"Are you the man they call *O Voador*?" a woman asked.

He was a handsome man and ladies gathered in droves around him, all of them radiant and witty and beseeching him to tutor them in the rudiments of science.

It was impossible not to be caught up in this festive atmosphere and soon I found myself dancing with a girl wearing a mask of black feathers. Later, we went to her box to amuse ourselves. She put virtuous protests to my embraces yet her obstacles were feeble and I disarmed her with exotic tales and gentle kisses. When I returned, merry and a little light-headed, to where my brother stood, I found him in conversation with a lady wearing a mask trimmed with lace.

"There is no cure for melancholy," I heard him say, "except to find God, or heaven, if it exists."

"Or love?" she said, rolling her glances toward me.

"A man must love what he does," Bartolomeu said.

"Monsieur is a recluse!"

"I'd prefer if madame would call me a man of reason."

"But reason is cold and rational," the lady replied, with bold familiarity. "If we are to believe in reason alone, then there would be no art, no books, no culture, no songs and no love."

"Reason will reveal to us the truth."

"But then we must live without hope!"

At that moment, I noticed a blue domino arrive in the doorway. I motioned to Bartolomeu and he turned to look at the death's-head, which glared at us majestically from across the room. Slowly, the domino began to make his way toward us. He came to where we stood and, opening a small door in the mirrored wall, ushered us into a dark corridor. We walked along the narrow passageway in silence until we arrived in a saloon with beautifully decorated walls and richly carved, gilded furniture. The paneled doors reached to the ceiling and a pair of guardsmen wearing the uniform of the Gendarmerie Nationale stood at attention on either side. As we entered, the domino pointed to a couple of chairs for us and sat down behind a walnut table.

He was young, not much older than I, but he carried himself with the air of a man twice his age. Even before he took off his mask, I knew he was the King.

"Father Bartolomeu, yes?" he said. "And this must be your brother? I have been expecting you gentlemen for some time. Were you going to pay your respects or was one to abandon hope?"

"Your Majesty!" Bartolomeu exclaimed, rising to his feet. "I had requested Monsieur Voltaire to arrange an audience but there are formalities in making a request and one must take one's place in the queue."

The King waved his hand in a dismissive gesture. "It is the gossip of Paris that you are a heretic fleeing the Inquisition," he continued. "By seeking refuge at the house of Voltaire, you are only giving color to this report. Men who are not in some sort of trouble with the church do not consort with that man."

"Are you a bearer of bad news, sire?" Bartolomeu asked, lowering his voice. "Is that why you wore a death's-head?"

"Oh, that was just an amusement," the King laughed. "Kingship is rather tedious, I find. I could have just sent for you but what's the pleasure in that? I wanted to see whether you'd come. I wanted to follow you and watch you."

"And what did you observe?"

"That you are a popular man, Father," said he, smiling. "I am sorry that I took you away from those adoring enchantresses."

"Am I to believe that they were sent by His Majesty?"

"If only you could be tempted so easily, Father."

The King laughed again. "It would appear that even Aphrodite would not stir your blood unless she came on silver wings."

"What do you intend to do with us?" Bartolomeu asked.

The King alternated between being melodramatic and pragmatic, but now he was no longer circumspect.

"I wish to extend to you the offer of my guardianship," he said.

"You don't intend to deport us to João V?"

"Oh, I'd keep you, in fact," he answered. "Had João V had some foresight, he might have fulfilled the prophecy of leading his nation into another golden age. No, I shan't deport you, for unlike in Portugal, the clock does not turn backward in France. The French nation can anticipate the great advantage of an airship. In fact, our greatest concern is that your machine falls into the hands of our inveterate enemies. I would insist that you be our guests."

§

SOON AFTER this interview, my brother and I found ourselves installed in a magnificent suite of apartments, with the King's maître d'hôtel himself assuming direct responsibility for our comforts. We were at liberty to fly the *Passarola* and conduct researches under the auspices of the King, who had become eagerly interested in the flying machine.

He had wide interests and did not care to exert his will over his wife or even his ministers. This lack of firmness made him a poor ruler, and perhaps a poor husband. He kept an irregular court, it is true, and history may judge him as a seducer and warmonger, but his reputation is only a consequence of fate. His character was far more intriguing. He was betrothed to the daughter of the exiled Polish king, Stanislaus Leszczyński, when he was fifteen years old; his matchmakers hoping that one day he might extend the influence of France by aiding his father-in-law in recovering the Polish throne. Maria Leszczyński turned out to be pious and plain. It was a loveless marriage and soon enough, Louis XV began to suffer from restlessness.

Phrases from the *philosophes* were constantly on his lips. He was prone to frequent bouts of melancholy, which he tried to assuage in the arms of his mistresses, but love was not the remedy. I believe that his moods were the consequence of forgoing his true calling. Someone once told me that he had been educated by Florentines and for a time he flirted with the idea of renouncing the throne to become an astronomer. The whim passed and he was persuaded to stay. The array of telescopes that he kept in his private observatory, pointing to the moons of Jupiter, were a constant reminder to him of how different life might have been—and his tendency to bring into the court his notes on celestial observations was probably the rem-nant of a habit that had lingered from his Floren-tine days.

In summer, he would set up his telescopes on the ship's deck and my brother or I would take him up on night flights to search for comets. In winter, the *Passarola* became his place of rendezvous. The ship would silently appear above the residence of one of his mistresses after midnight; he would throw a pebble against the window by arrangement agreed on beforehand and lower the ladder. The lady would climb up and the ship sail away, leaving no one the wiser. Sometimes, he also took his cats on these trysts, but the creatures suffered because of the cold air. So apart from transforming my cabin into a pillow-strewn boudoir for the King, fur-lined baskets in red and blue had to be installed for his cats. Bartolomeu offered to smuggle him out to somewhere like Naples or Florence, where he could live incognito for the rest of his life, but a fear of facing his destiny, I think, always prompted a retreat.

I must now turn my pen to other events, but before I part with my vignettes, I must remark that the time we spent in Paris was one of the happiest periods in my life. When I think of those years now, I recall that the passage of time itself had a languid quality about it and a weight and dimension that eludes me now. It made our stay seem a magical sojourn. The pleasure of having money to spend, the luncheons, drawn out into the afternoon and interspersed with chess, the hours of idleness, spent browsing in the cryptlike vaults of the Académie des Sciences, the pleasure of planning adventures on board the *Passarola*—departing to the Indies one year, Africa the next—and perhaps foremost, the blessing of being young in a new country: these joys erased my sorrows as if such things had never existed. I recall this time as one long season of masquerades, balls, card games, garden parties and operas. Paris was beautiful. In Lisbon, the beauty of the palaces and churches vanishes as you approach the

white stone; but the buildings of Paris looked splendid from a distance and just as beautiful up close,
adorned with every kind of ornament. The women
were well bred, the courtesans gentle, the men polite, and the children well mannered. Although, of
course, we must have had our share of cold winters,
my recollection is of an eternal summer. ❦

# { 13 }

I T WAS a cold and crisp April morning when Bartolomeu and I were summoned to the King's
study. A fire blazed in the great marble fireplace. The
walls were lined with bookcases, some as tall as the
ceiling and others with marble busts on them. A
small group of officers in blue uniforms was gathered around a green billiard table, poring over military charts and papers. The red velvet curtains were
drawn from the windows and Louis XV himself
stood with his back to us, looking out at the garden.

"Don't you love the garden in the mornings?" the
King said after we had been announced. "The
frosted terraces, the green yew... splashed with violet, purple and white. Everything is clean and
pure. Every blade stands out in the golden light,

crisp and clear, as if painted by a master. The cold absorbs all sound. You tread on the pebbles but even the crunch of your footsteps is muffled by the silence. I especially love the birds. The sparrows and tits . . . they are like children. They flock to the fountain and they come to my windows and peck on the glass for their due. I give them oatmeal and cooked rice. They like the rice. They are so much like human beings, you see. Once they develop a taste for something, they won't touch anything else."

The King now turned to us and sighed. "Forgive me if I wax lyrical, gentlemen," he remarked in Portuguese. "My feathered friends bring out the poet in me. *C'est ma faiblesse.* I am glad you could come. It is not my fashion to send for my guests at this hour but a great crisis has arisen. Captain Suchet here will explain why you've been called."

A smart young officer stepped forward and started bombarding us with details of the Polish succession. The matter of the succession became an immediate concern early in the year, when the elderly king passed away. Stanislaus Leszczyński was elected king and his departure from Versailles celebrated by a magnificent fête. The exiles showed much joy at the prospect of returning home in his wake and even crowds of Parisians came out in the streets to bid him farewell. But when he entered Warsaw, he found that the Austrians and the Russians had forced the Poles to accept their favored candidate. Cossacks appeared at the gates and, unable to resist them, Stanislaus fled, twelve days after his election, to the coastal town of Danzig. The Russians pursued him. They besieged Danzig and pounded the stronghold with cannon fire. A French fleet was sent to break the siege. The ships disembarked an army of a little over two thousand men but it could do nothing against the Russian might of twenty thousand and was forced to surrender.

"We had hoped to maintain a balance of power against the Austrians and the Russians but our plans are thwarted and their ambition already realized," the captain surmised. "We will not be able to resist a concentrated attack on the city's defenses. It's only a matter of time before Danzig falls. The peril is increasing every day. We need to send someone secretly to Poland to rescue Stanislaus before the Russians capture him."

The King returned to the billiard table and looked gravely at Bartolomeu. "Father, how fast is your ship?"

"How fast, Your Majesty?" Bartolomeu echoed. "We traveled from Lisbon to Paris—a distance of nine hundred miles—in three nights."

"Tell me, what would it take for you to make sail to Danzig?"

"It'll take money, Your Majesty," Bartolomeu observed, "for repairs: the sails need to be stitched, there's caulking to be done and new rigging is required."

"Anything else?"

"We'd be risking our lives."

"Can the ship carry cannons?" the captain asked.

Bartolomeu stared at the man momentarily. "Is this a rescue mission or an assignment to attack the enemy?"

"We may send you back on combat duty," the captain replied. "The possibility has not been ruled out."

"I think you are being a little presumptuous," Bartolomeu chuckled. "I am not a soldier and I don't take orders."

It was obvious that the two men had disliked each other from the moment they met. Each recognized in the other a man of a totally different kind.

"Father, I could order my men to seize your vessel," the captain snarled.

"Oh? And who will fly it? You?"

"We can make you fly," said he. He spoke with the tone that I have always found so coarse in men of his profession—that customary disdain of a soldier for civilians.

"And how exactly will you persuade me?"

"We have our ways."

Bartolomeu rose and shook his head. "If I am to be threatened then I no longer wish to continue this conversation."

"Where are you going?"

"I shall go where I please."

The captain raised his voice. "Don't forget that you are a guest in this country."

"Am I to be reminded of my obligations?"

"Your limitations, Father," the captain said. "You are not a French citizen. You are a foreigner, suspected of crimes aboard. We know what you want to do."

"Ah, you are also a clairvoyant?" Bartolomeu said.

"You wish to escape. You want to fly free. I tell you that you will fly when and where we tell you to fly."

"Well then, if I am such a bad man, arrest me now," Bartolomeu said, glancing around at the assembly. "What are you waiting for?"

No one else spoke.

"Captain, you must drop this talk!" the King said after a long silence, no doubt after having weighed and watched the contest with cold, dispassionate eyes. "Your kind only sees one way to go about things. I am not about to threaten anyone. Father Bartolomeu, I am sure, is an intelligent man who realizes the rewards of a successful mission."

Then he turned around and addressed my brother. "Father, it is not usual for me to ask my guests for favors, but we live in unusual times which call for unusual measures. The capture of my father-in-law will be our humiliation. I cannot let it stain my country's honor. I hope you understand this. Of course, I only ask if you would *wish* to volunteer for the mission. We are a civilized people. I certainly do not intend to conscript you."

Bartolomeu took me to one side, out of earshot of the others. He told me that he was willing to take the commission even though he did not like the tone of the proceedings. He could scarcely afford to refuse the King himself and besides, the undertaking, if successful, was certain to provide us with much vaunted privileges.

I knew though that he was willing for reasons far more visceral than he cared to admit.

"You need not explain," I said. "Would an opium eater ever refuse the drug?"

He grinned. "Where do you stand?" he asked plainly.

I was idle. I had been enjoying the comforts of my Parisian life but there was little variety in my pleasures. I dreamt of severities and wanted to experience danger.

"I am with you," I said.

He clapped my shoulder and we returned to join the others. The King bade us to the table.

"Danzig lies some eight hundred miles northeast of Paris," he said, pointing at the chart. "How long will that take you?"

Bartolomeu frowned. "Everything depends on weather," he said. "With a favorable wind, we could cover the distance in two or three days."

"With bad weather?"

He shrugged. "Who knows? A week..."

"Father," said the King, "you'll make preparations immediately. My men will provide you with whatever you need—food, guns, powder, everything. You'll depart in ten days...a week...no...you shall leave the day after tomorrow. The captain will see to it."

As we were about to leave, the King's mood changed suddenly. A moment ago, he was acting like a monarch; now he became lost in his thoughts and his voice softened.

"Father, I saw an arctic tern today," he said. "I think I saw her last year, or maybe one of her kind. I cannot tell. Tomorrow she'll be gone perhaps and who knows whether she'll come next year. She follows the same path all her life and then she dies. Can you imagine living the same life if you were reborn?"

"I would live it as I've lived it now."

"Every moment of it?"

"Even this conversation."

"Then you can't have too many regrets," the King said wistfully. "I myself crave nothing more than a different life." ℮

# { 14 }

T HE FLIGHT to Danzig was without incident. The weather was fair and the *Passarola* served us well. Our instructions were to sail under the cover of darkness, land our ship near an agreed landmark, bring Stanislaus on board and leave. The landmark was supposed to be a large bonfire lit within the fortress. But when we arrived over Danzig, we saw that there were dozens of large and small bonfires burning in and around the township. Which one was ours? We descended to five hundred feet but it was a dark and moonless night. We heard soldiers singing around campfires but could see nothing. We made one pass over the lines out to the shoreline, then descended a hundred feet for another pass, and then a third at treetop height.

"Do you see them?" Bartolomeu asked me each time in a voice that was becoming more anxious.

By this time, several hours had passed. The wind from the sea had a sting in it. My hands were already frozen and despite the oilskins, I felt the cold seeping into my bones. Below us, the bonfires were going out one after the other. The singing slowly petered out into drunken sobs. The sky grew lighter and we began to hear the first volleys of musket fire. A mantle of fog lay low over the ground. Before the sun rose, it started to glow white and, within its silvery haze, we saw the ancient battlement towers standing tall along the coast. A solitary bonfire was burning on a raised hillock. It was ours. A sentry waved at us and, as we passed over the ramparts, we saw the faces of French soldiers. This was followed by a popping sound below us—musket fire from the Russians.

Our landing site was an open space within the fortress where several dozen armed soldiers were standing in small groups. I looked at them as we descended. They watched us with expressions that varied from suspicion to awe to apathy; the general manifestation was indeed apathy. Officers and men alike looked slovenly and blue from the cold. A few had grown beards but most of the faces I saw were young. While a few stragglers loitered around the ship, the others soon lost interest and went about their own business.

After we secured our ship, we were taken to a guardhouse. From its narrow windows we could see the French and Polish battlements extending along the coast to our left, and the Russian lines stretching from the base of the fortress out to a slope and onto the hills, where the Russians had placed heavy guns behind earthen redoubts. The ground below us teemed with enemy troops. There were thousands and thousands of bivouacs and while those nearby were deserted, the occupants farther afield were cleaning their guns, squatting around campfires, washing, spitting and going about their everyday life as if they were still in barracks somewhere in the steppes.

One hour passed, and another. The church bells rang. Our soldiers threw their slop into the green water of the moat and the rotting smell of garbage and excrement clung to my nostrils.

Eight o'clock came and suddenly a trumpet blew. A sentry posted outside stood at attention as a young lieutenant came on horse galloping down the road.

*"Vive le roi! Vive la reine!"* He saluted as he entered our room. "His Majesty will be here any minute. Are you ready?"

Bartolomeu said that we were.

"Very well. You ought to fly him to one of our ships anchored beyond the harbor," he said. "A frigate could take him back to France. It's not safe for him to travel with you in the airship. He is not well."

Bartolomeu and I exchanged a few words. Our instructions were to evacuate Stanislaus but they did not specify how we brought him back to Paris. The lieutenant's suggestion seemed like wise counsel and we thanked him for it.

Then in a quiet manner, almost blushing, he impressed upon us that he was from the Flanders regiment and a nephew of the Duke of Orléans. Was there room on board for him?

"You don't have to commend yourself to us," Bartolomeu said to him in a gentle, kindly voice. "Even if you were the King's cousin, we could not take you. The ship is not designed to fly with any more passengers on board. The Russians will shoot us down before we gain any height."

After trying to persuade us more formally, he finally begged us to take him home because his mother was sick. It was not easy to put him off but when he went away, we watched him walk down the rampart. Some men called out after him but he hastened his steps, turned around a tower and disappeared.

"Did you see his face?" Bartolomeu asked me after he was gone. "A mere boy. It is a children's army they have gathered here. I ought to return him to his mother and leave Stanislaus behind."

With this, he pulled out a hip flask and a small tin can from his satchel. "I should have never become involved in this infernal matter," he said, pouring himself a drink. "But now that we are neck deep in it, I don't fancy us being killed for anyone's sake."

A ball struck the outer walls of our guardhouse and showered us with falling plaster. He handed me another can, poured out some wine and raised his can for a toast.

"Here's to luck," he said. "Ha!"

It was past nine o'clock when Stanislaus finally arrived. He was a polite gray-haired gentleman whom I would have taken for a lawyer or an astronomer were it not for the circumstances. "Who ordered my rescue?" he demanded. "I don't wish to go back. Is this an intrigue?" He continued to protest as his hosts pushed him on board the *Passarola* and untied our ropes.

The ship began to rise. We looked below at the men who had come to bid farewell as the ground pulled away.

"*Au revoir*, then!" Stanislaus cried out.

"It's *adieu*, Your Highness!" one of the lieutenants shouted back. 'You won't see us again.' It was the same young man who had asked us to smuggle him aboard. Tears were running down his face.

We rose quickly and turned in a northeasterly direction to rendezvous with the French ships. Stanislaus sat huddled on the deck. He refused to stand up and when he finally did rise, he tottered and grasped at anything like a man without his sea legs. It was amusing watching him; he would stare right ahead, or up at the sky, but he would not look below, keeping himself well back from the gunwales. It was when the gunfire started that his curiosity finally overcame him. He edged close to me, held the gunwale with both hands and leant over.

The bay was covered with Russian ships. They lay at anchor. From our height, we could see little activity on their decks but the lookouts must have spotted us, for we heard hoarse cries of "*Frantsuzy*! Kill, kill!" Soon after, the thud of musket fire began.

"Right to helm," Bartolomeu shouted as I wrestled with the rigging and pushed out the boom. "Steady!"

He was watching the ships like a hawk. Stanislaus observed him for a while and when Bartolomeu did not make any conversation, he went to my brother and asked if we could steer the vessel back over enemy lines.

Bartolomeu shook his head. "Those are not my orders," he said.

Stanislaus raised his eyebrows. "You intend to disobey me?"

"I take my orders from the King of France," Bartolomeu said. "I have His Majesty's commission in my pocket."

"You know how easily we can defeat them from the air?" Stanislaus said after a pause. "As for gunpowder, there's plenty there, I think; or should we perhaps take some musketeers on board? We may lose some but we would kill scores."

"The *Passarola* is not a warship," my brother said, peering through the telescope. By the way he spoke and the tone of his voice, it was plain to me that he was in earnest.

Stanislaus looked at him as if he was taking his measure. "Doesn't your heart quicken a little to think that your airship might change the course of nations?"

"It's all vanity as far as I can see."

"Father, I have waited twenty-four years to reclaim my crown. A man must meet his fate, you must know that."

Bartolomeu smiled. "It appears that that man is also a king without a crown."

There was a gleam in Stanislaus's eyes. "There is no honor in exile," he said.

"Isn't there?"

"Of course not. What's a man without his country?"

"Exile has freed me from a great deal of trouble," my brother said, glancing at me. "I am still alive, as is my brother. We both still have our heads on our shoulders. I cannot say so much of many others who have fallen into the arms of the Inquisition."

"Bah! To flee from trouble, to keep no attachments, to have no anchors and to live in the pay of foreigners—what sort of existence is that?"

"Does a sailor ever concern himself with what happens on land?" Bartolomeu replied. "Once you become accustomed to the wind, the heights and the immense infinity of the sky, nothing is more fulfilling than this life. Why should I worry about politics and world affairs? They are a digression. I like my distance from things."

He looked through the telescope one last time and passed it to Stanislaus. "It lends enchantment to the view."

Stanislaus put the telescope to his eye. "You can't have too many cares then," he remarked and turned the instrument to where Bartolomeu was pointing.

We were now some two-thirds of the way between the Russian and the French frigates. Three of the French ships lay anchored several miles out north by northwest. To the east, the yellow coast was slowly edging away. Plumes of smoke hung lazily over the distant fortress but the roar of the sea drowned out the sound of gunfire. The Russian soldiers, small and toylike, were inching toward a breach, their bayonets glinting in the sun. The scene seemed like a tableau from a puppet theater, with the marionettes slowly moving forward in unison, as if pulled along by strings. Then a flock of gulls passed between us and them, breaking the spell.

"Are you expecting an assault?" Bartolomeu asked.

"The Russians have been preparing for it for days," Stanislaus sighed. "I can see that it has begun."

"Then your army ought to surrender."

"We intend to join battle and stand our ground to the man."

"You can hold out for a week or two but what difference will it make?" Bartolomeu shrugged. "Your men are outnumbered. They will die like dogs."

"We'll give them a bloody nose before they push us into the sea," Stanislaus said, but he looked, and sounded, beaten.

Meanwhile, the wind shifted to the south and we were blown to the bay once again. The Russian ships were four or five hundred feet below, their decks now swarming with sailors. Some of the men had clambered onto the platforms halfway up the masts, where they started firing at us. Puffs of white smoke began to appear below. Fortunately we were out of range but a few stray shots whistled past. I attempted to fire back but the wind buffeted the *Passarola* and all my shots went amiss.

"I would rather fight my foes on the ground than have them cracking shots at me up here," Stanislaus remarked over the gunfire.

"That's bravely said for a king who flies away with his rear to his enemies," my brother said, laughing.

Stanislaus flushed red.

"You think I am a coward?"

"I think you ought to have settled your feud and saved the lives of the men who are now going to die for it."

"Did I ever ask to be rescued?" returned Stanislaus, drawing out his own pistol. "I am a patriot. It wouldn't have crossed my mind."

I thought that my brother's taunts had coaxed him into firing at the enemy below, only to discover that he was pointing the gun at us.

"Turn the ship around," he cried. "We are going ashore."

Suddenly, there was a loud metallic clang. The ship shook violently. The Pole stumbled and the weapon fell out of his hands. I turned around to see that Bartolomeu's face was ashen. Greatly alarmed, I called out to him but when he made no reply, I noticed that his eyes were staring at something over my shoulder. I turned my head, and shall never forget the feeling of helplessness that chilled me to the marrow of my bones when I realized that one of the spheres had burst.

The ship began to spin, gradually at first and then faster by turns. Bartolomeu clambered up the mast and hastened to furl the sail.

"You better start throwing the sandbags overboard, sir," he shouted at Stanislaus. "Because I won't have any qualms now about throwing *you* overboard!"

I did not hear the rest as the wind drowned out his voice.

Stanislaus rose from the floor, pale and unsteady, and lifted the sandbags one by one, edging them over the gunwale. The feeble effort scarcely slowed our fall.

"That was a bad job," I remarked.

"I'm sorry about what I did," he replied with a trembling voice. "I never meant to harm you or put your ship in danger."

"Oh, it's already done," I said angrily, and with these words, started throwing out whatever I could lay my hands on—anchors, rigging, even our weapons I hurled away, but to no avail: the ship plunged toward its watery grave. The sea loomed closer and closer. A gust of air filled up our sails and buoyed us momentarily; we rose a little and covered some distance before the wind flagged again and the sails flapped. For a moment, the *Passarola* remained suspended, as if dangling on a string. I felt a sickly tightness in the pit of my stomach. An irrepressible desire forced me to stare at the waves below. I wondered, without feeling, about the sensations of a drowning man. Then the ship began to tumble down faster and faster; the spray caught us and we crashed.

In that violent plunge, I fell overboard. I have a vague memory of finding myself drawn down under the waves before a few strong kicks brought me to the surface again. My principal fear was sharks. I had a wild image of the depths below me teeming with the monsters and in order to escape from their jaws, I swam vigorously toward the stricken ship. I have no doubt that I ever swam faster in my life. I reached the side of the vessel and quickly hauled myself on board, imagining the sea behind me foaming with the indignant creatures, except in reality, it was dull and gray and there was not a single fin in sight.

Bartolomeu pulled me aboard. The waves washed over the gunwales and the wrecked ship rolled and pitched in them like a log. We were all on our feet, bailing hard, but I could feel that we were gradually sinking. The hatches were shut but the hull was breached; the deck was split open and every now and then, a large wave drove it beneath the water. Soon the ship was leaning to one side and its bow was completely submerged. We lashed ourselves to the poop deck, which still showed above the waves, and clung to the hull in silence, wondering whether we should be drowned before friend or foe could reach us. We lay close together. Shortly afterward, the sea became calmer and Stanislaus spoke, asking my brother if he thought there was any prospect of our being saved. Bartolomeu lay with his face pressed against the hull, the water washing over him and when he remained silent, I feared that he had drowned, but presently, he raised his head; the pain on his face was evident.

"Aren't you glad to be away from the horrors of the fortress?"

"I am grateful," Stanislaus replied, "but our trials are not over yet."

"Trials! Tell me not of trials," Bartolomeu said grimly. "My trials are over. My ship is wrecked. There's no more life in her than the dead rolling of the waves; if she sinks, then shackle me to her side and send me to the bottom." ❦

# { 15 }

W E ROLLED in the swell for perhaps an hour before a masthead appeared on the horizon. Stanislaus saw it first and hailed the sight with rapturous shouts. The ship was bearing down upon us and we feared the Russians, having seen us, had sent one of their ships in pursuit; but as it neared, we saw that it was one of the French frigates. Bartolomeu was greatly relieved but it was Stanislaus and I who celebrated with ecstatic joy. We cheered and screamed and shouted at the top of our voices, waving madly at the vessel as it drew near.

The frigate stopped some distance away and lowered two jolly boats, which set out in our direction. Once we were pulled aboard one of these, several sailors left their seats, rolled up their trousers and scrambled over the *Passarola*'s capsized hull. They tied the mauled airship fast to the boats with coils of rope; all hands heaved at the oars and in this manner, the two boats towed the wreck in tandem back to the frigate. The sailors explained how several men on the deck had followed the flight of the *Passarola* as she set out from the coast. They had had no inkling of what it was that they were seeing but when they saw the Russians open fire, they knew that the contraption was theirs. The lookout raised the alarm when she fell out of the sky and the frigate set out immediately to search for survivors.

It was more than an hour after being taken on board the *Spartiate* before we were summoned to the captain's cabin. His name was de Conflans. He had a scar under his left eye and limped with his right leg as he swung out from behind his table to greet us.

"Your Majesty!" he doffed his hat at Stanislaus. "I had heard that a rescue attempt was afoot. Of course, one hears more and more rumors as a battle is about to be lost and one simply cannot believe them, especially when they entail a flying machine and aviators. But now I have seen it all with my own eyes."

He shook my hand briefly and then came to stand in front of my brother.

"*O Voador*, I presume?"

"Captain!"

"It is an honor. I trust that you'll find passage aboard my sixty-four-gun ship safe. Now, you all must be dead tired, I fancy—yes? Why not have a stiff glass of rum and I'll tell the boys to swing hammocks for you."

"I'd like to see my ship first," Bartolomeu said.

"Ah, like a groom pining for his bride," the captain remarked. "Your ship is safe, sir."

"Where is she?"

"Moored alongside the *Spartiate*," the captain replied. "Two beauties in sweet embrace, their fates yoked together in iron."

Suddenly we heard a cry from the masthead. The captain was out of the door in a flash and a moment later, we were all gathered on the deck around him, our faces turned up.

"Sail ho!" the lookout cried, pointing toward the coastal waters. A wave of excitement rippled through the crew.

"What does she look like?" the captain shouted.

"A Russian, sir!"

We began peering in that direction and soon could make out the topsails of a ship coming over the horizon. The topgallant sails then appeared, the royals and jib and spanker and soon we could see the entire frigate gaining upon us. Her sides were painted with stripes of white, blue and red, and as the wind was blowing in our direction, we could hear the sound of drums. All in all, she seemed like a formidable opponent.

"Sail ho!" the lookout cried again.

This time there were murmurs and cries of astonishment. The men were not afraid of the first frigate—they were indeed spoiling for a fight—but an encounter with two frigates was most unwelcome. A shadow fell over their spirits.

"Masthead?"

"Another Russian, sir!" the ensign replied.

A few moments later, a lieutenant passed us his telescope and we saw her too. She was painted black and lying to under topsails. Her taut white canvas sails, brilliant in the sun, bore a colossal coat of arms of the double-headed eagle. We were standing with de Conflans on the quarterdeck watching the maneuvers of our two opponents. They were some thousand yards from us when they raised their standards; we raised ours and began preparations for the fight.

"Put her *hors de combat!*" the captain shouted to his quartermasters. Then he lit his pipe and began smoking furiously. My recollection of what passed next is confused. Stanislaus was taken below deck but no one took any notice of Bartolomeu and me. We stood on the quarterdeck, in direct line of sight of our foes. There was a melee of men around me and I soon lost sight of my brother. I felt brave and foolish and thrilled with the flutter of apprehension—that convulsion in the pit of my stomach that I've only felt when in grave danger. I felt fear but I had no hesitation to face battle. It was a heady feeling, an intoxicating combination of great terror and, I daresay, pleasure.

At six hundred yards, the first Russian frigate began firing her guns. The cannonballs arched through the air and fell harmlessly into the water between the closing ships, spraying water over us. The striped frigate slowly turned alongside with its broadside aimed at our larboard. It was so near that I could see the faces of the sailors, but before that ship anchored, de Conflans turned and passed close to her stern, raking it with grapeshot and mowing down the men at their posts. Our crew cheered but the celebration was brief because the *Spartiate* was caught between her fire on the larboard quarter and the other frigate's guns on the starboard bow. The flashes from their muzzles, the whistling noise and the explosions around us increased. Shots were screeching over our heads, making a tearing sound as they flew past, as if they were ripping the fabric of air itself. A twenty-pounder exploded in the forecastle; it must have struck a pig in the sty, for we heard a squeal. Then that awful sound was drowned out by other horrid noises—a thud behind us where an ensign fell, shot away; the shrieks and cries of the wounded; splinters flying over my head. Then our batteries opened up—a whole line of flame spat out from the gun ports on my right. I winced. My heart was beating like a bird's. Scattered thoughts ran through my mind. The folly of the entire trip came to me now all at once. My blood ran cold to think that Bartolomeu might already be dead. I called out his name but he did not show himself. My cries were drowned out in the noise and I was left wondering what I ought to do and where I ought to go. One moment, I wanted to hide in the hold, but I heard someone shout that we had been struck below the waterline; another moment, I wanted to man a carronade on the quarterdeck, stripped to the waist like the sailors, but I could not summon my body to rise. Fear had frozen me. My senses remained alert but I could not move my arms or legs. The rumble of cannons became a continuous din and I could no longer tell who was firing at whom. Every now and again, I felt the *Spartiate* shudder like an ox bitten by a scorpion and I knew that we had been hit.

§

WHEN I raised my head again, I saw dead and wounded everywhere. Another ensign dangled from the rigging. Streaks of blood covered the deck. A man's leg was nearly shot off. He was carried down to the ward to have it amputated. Another man lay cut in two. I saw the sailors throw his remains overboard. But the most astonishing spectacle I saw was the captain, pacing the deck as if it were a promenade, and the shots flying around him no more than autumn leaves. I remember my impression—he was cheering his men and telling them to fix their attention solely on the carronade while the dead were being thrown overboard.

I do not know how long the battle lasted. Perhaps half an hour, perhaps several hours. When in mortal danger, one exists outside of time. Seconds, minutes, hours melt away. One's senses awaken so that even a brief moment seems a great deal longer afterward. In any event, a considerable period must have lapsed and there was still no sign of the other French frigates. The three ships were running parallel to one another, with the *Spartiate* caught between the Russian frigates; but de Conflans would not be pounded into submission. The captain had maneuvered the *Spartiate* so deftly that neither ship could fire a broadside into us without running the risk of hitting the other. In this mayhem, the *Spartiate* gained a position under the stern of the striped frigate and on an uproll, aimed her fire amidships. The shot struck. The enemy's mizzenmast was hit. A fire started in the stern. We saw the other ship close its hatches and move away and soon realized the cause—the fire was near the magazine. Men were jumping overboard from the stricken ship and yelling out for help.

The *Spartiate* turned around and sailed out. There was nothing we could do. We must have been some three hundred yards from the doomed vessel when it blew up with a tremendous explosion. A pillar of smoke arose and stood still for a long time. Whole chunks of ship flew through the air in every direction. The rudder cartwheeled over our heads and splashed near our stern. Blazing bits of splinters fell all around. When the smoke finally cleared, we saw that the ship's entire deck and much of its forecastle had been blown to bits. All that remained in its place was a burning hulk above the waterline.

The battle had been won. The other ship was withdrawing and we had a clear passage to the sea. I stood at the stern as we made sail, for I could not pull myself away from the spectacle in our wake. A moment later, Bartolomeu appeared and came to stand beside me. He was unhurt. We were both greatly relieved and we unburdened ourselves first by upbraiding and then by embracing each other. I learnt that he had spent the entire battle tucked away in the stern of the hold, sitting in pitch darkness with mice scuttling about him and hearing nothing except for the din of guns above. The scenes of horror that he now saw appalled him. I too was distressed but had had a change of heart. I was far more troubled by the perils and presumptions of our chosen occupation. Seeing him thoughtful, I made up my mind to tell him of my doubts.

"How long are we going to be mercenaries?" I exclaimed.

"As long as it pays for our vocation," he said.

"*Your* vocation," I replied, feeling frustrated that despite all that we had been through, he had had no second thoughts. "I'm finished with flying."

"So your mind's made up on that?"

I said that it was.

He gave me a thin smile. "You're certainly contrary."

I did not reply.

"Don't you want to rise above all this?"

"All what?" I said.

"You don't see?"

"No."

"Earthly things. That corpse floating there— whose son was he? Those corpses below—how many fathers and husbands lie drowned there? And that man whose entrails splattered on the deck— were his parents proud of him once? Don't you want to lift yourself up—away from all this misery?"

"It's in our nature," I said. "We'll take it with us wherever we go."

Dead bodies floated in the water, scorched and half naked. The water foamed where sharks rolled in the blood, tossing the carcasses from side to side in their great jaws—and I could not even tell if the dead were ours or the Russians'. A pistol shot brought me out of my reverie: the pig stopped squealing. ❦

# { 16 }

THE REMAINDER of the *Spartiate*'s journey was safe and uneventful. I volunteered for the decks for the duration and life agreed well with me on the foretop. A few weeks later, we disembarked at Brest. We lost track of our companions soon after but there was occasional news. I heard that the *Spartiate* saw action off the Canadian coast, where the ship engaged English men-of-war in a fatal battle. The captain died with his last wish fulfilled. He sank an English frigate, but canister shot killed him. His body was weighed down with cannonballs, sewn inside a canvas sail and lowered into the sea.

As for Stanislaus, I heard of him again at Königsberg, where he formed a confederation and sent an envoy to Versailles asking Louis XV to invade Saxony. His partisans ultimately scattered and in 1736, he abdicated the throne. He eventually settled in Lunéville with his mistress, Madame de Boufflers and spent the rest of his life dedicated to science and philosophy. He corresponded with Rousseau and occasionally with my brother. I also heard that he became a winemaker of some repute. His last years were happy and the vintage of 1766, the year he died, was supposedly exceptional.

But the main consequence of this adventure was that the *Passarola* no longer flew. The crash and the naval battle had wrecked it. Its hull was shattered, its rigging cut to pieces, its sails riddled with holes, and the copper spheres pierced by splinters. The French had no objections to paying for the repairs but everything was bogged down in bureaucracy. When Bartolomeu made a fuss about tardiness, the administrators decided he was a troublemaker and set about punishing him with more delays. Sometimes the funds became scarce and sometimes materials were hard to come by. The administrators even set up committees to make certain that the ship was being refitted according to the best practices of the trade—this being governed by men who had no idea of flight.

I suspect that the real cause of our plight was the King's displeasure at my brother's row with Stanislaus. We could not see him because he was occupied elsewhere, we were told, and with Voltaire in Lorraine, we had few friends left in the capital. We felt betrayed and forgotten. It was not a pleasant time. The language, the brilliance of the saloons and those very charms of Paris that had appealed so much to me before now seemed foreign and meaningless. I kept mistresses and took new ones when I pleased. There was always the scent of a noblewoman in my bed, but despite my affairs, I felt lonely. Maria came into my dreams and asked me why I had deserted her and I awoke with the depressing thought that I had failed in some deep and profound way.

Bartolomeu distracted himself by compiling dossiers of his notes and ship logs. He predicted the return of Halley's comet in the middle of the century and added thirteen new objects to his list of comets. The Lourenço dossier, as it was known, became the most comprehensive list of comets in the Northern Hemisphere. Aside from his scientific work, he speculated on cognition and wrote a monograph entitled *Theoria philosophiae naturalis*, in which he suggested that leisure was a necessary condition to think.

When the monograph was published, Voltaire is said to have laughed in ridicule. "If one needs leisure to think," he remarked, "then why is our leisured class so foolish?"

Bartolomeu began to suspect that everyone was intriguing against him. The loss of the *Passarola* made him feel like an invalid. He slunk away from society and fell behind in fashions and gossip, which made it only more difficult for him to be considered acceptable again. He had little to say to others and no interest in what they had to tell, unless the matter related to flying machines. Only then did his voice lift and his eyes sparkle, and when the topic of conversation changed again—as it did so frequently—he fell into a torpor again. When he appeared at some fête, which was rare, he loitered alone. I remember one instance when he cornered Monsieur de Soubise, admiral of the navy, and tried to persuade him that if France invaded Austria with an armada of flying ships, the gendarmes could descend from the sky and take Vienna. The old statesman, perhaps embarrassed by Bartolomeu's lack of tact, for France and Austria were enjoying a brief peace, mumbled something about the spirit of the treaty and excused himself.

The desire to cast himself away became so great that Bartolomeu began to disappear from Paris for weeks. Only I knew that he traveled by chaise to Piedmont or La Ferriere to walk alone in the Alps. Climbing the dazzling walls of ice was not pleasurable but the thrill, the fear of succumbing to nature's elements, was, perhaps the nearest thing to flying. But each time he returned invigorated by the highlands, the lowlands soon drained him and he had to flee again.

§

THEN ONE day, quite suddenly, we were summoned to the King's private chamber. I had been here several times before but the impression of comfort and splendor never failed to astonish me. Rich carpets lay scattered upon the polished floors. On the walls, sketches of the pyramids and the desert alternated with paintings of ships and birds. A crusader's iron sword hung above the fireplace while Moorish shields made from rhinoceros skin flanked the windows. In the center of this room was a mahogany desk, with rosewood and ebony parquetry, covered with mathematical tables, maps, wineglasses and pencils. There were no flowers, nothing soft or feminine to balance the untidy masculine atmosphere of the place.

There were two men in the room: the King and a visitor, who introduced himself as Pierre-Louis Moreau de Maupertuis from the Académie des Sciences. In appearance and stature, he seemed to be in his thirties, perhaps a few years older than my brother but there was something about his face which made him look a great deal older. He had gray bristles flaring at his temples and a large forehead, such as a mathematician or logician might have. Louis XV indicated a couple of armchairs and handed us a cedar box filled with the long, slim barrels of Spanish cigars.

"Do you know this map, Father?" he asked Bartolomeu, pointing to a chart on the wall.

"It's the Cosmographie Universelle by Guillaume le Testu."

"Precisely. Now look at it closely, Father," the King asked. "What do you see?"

"The Terra Australis, sire," Bartolomeu replied.

"And what does that name mean to you?"

"It is the mythical southern continent, of course, of which Ptolemy has spoken and that Columbus believed to be a lush green land flowing with rivers and populated by people who wear clothes of gold leaf."

The question had been a test and I could see that Bartolomeu had not answered it correctly. The King seemed disappointed. "What it shows is paradise—a land of happiness. It shows hope, that map, Father. That's why I like maps. I like them with sea monsters and mermaids. I like them with dragons and centaurs. I like them more if they are incomplete and incorrect—for then the chance of discovery is even greater. The fog lifts and a new cape looms into view...ah, what sailor would not risk his life for such a sight?"

"There is no thrill in life without living for utopias, is there?" his guest remarked, looking at us.

The King looked at him with mock disapproval. "Maupertuis is a contrary man," he said, drawing out a cigar. "He says one thing and does another. He wants to draw maps which strike out utopias. Is that not so?"

"All things in their correct dimensions, sire," Maupertuis replied.

"'Tis the Age of Reason," the King sighed, "but one thing is clear to me and that is that if our ships are to rule the waves, then our maps must be true depictions of the world. Father, what do you know of the figure of the earth?"

"Opinions vary, Your Majesty," Bartolomeu shrugged, "depending on whom you believe."

"Whom do you believe?" he asked.

"Myself, I follow Sir Isaac Newton, who has demonstrated that the world is a sphere flattened toward the poles."

The King smiled through the haze of smoke and looked at his guest. "Then you have found a companion here who is also an admirer of the English. But I need not remind you that we are in France, where we like to believe a Frenchman. As you are aware, our own Monsieur Cassini thinks the earth is a sphere elongated toward the poles. The question in my mind, gentlemen, is, where lies the truth?"

The visitor told us that the figure of a flat sphere or an elongated one gave very different distances for places that had the same longitude and latitude, a matter of some concern to navigators. What we did not know was that the debate had merited the attention of the Académie and it had decided to equip two expeditions to set sail to the Equator and the Polar Circle, to measure the length of the meridian so that the comparison between them would determine the earth's exact figure.

"But the length of a degree is already known," Bartolomeu remarked, looking at his host. "Fernel, Snellius and Riccioli have all calculated it."

"They are inaccurate," the visitor replied; "therefore, all of our charts and maps are inaccurate. They show islands where there are none and waterways where there are reefs. The mistakes are only small but even a difference of a seventh part of a degree can cause a shipwreck."

"Father, I'm prepared to ensure that your airship is quickly repaired, but on one condition. I need men," he said, darting a glance in my direction, "young men who can accomplish the task in the shortest possible time. If a ship is fitted out to sail to the Baltic Sea and the men venture out on land thereafter, it'll be at least a year before they return. The *Passarola* would accomplish the same task in a matter of months."

"I am not an adventurer, Your Majesty."

"Your flight from Danzig was as fine a tale of adventure as I have ever heard."

"I am finished with it."

The King looked at him with arched eyebrows. "You are finished with flying?" he asked.

"I've taken enough risks."

"Oh, so am I to believe that you will scuttle your ship and grow roses?"

"I do not plan to retire," Bartolomeu said, coloring at this rejoinder.

"Ah, I see!" the King exclaimed, a smile of reproof on his lips. "You are going to join a circus and give joyrides to people. Would you have a stall in St. Germain or do you plan to go on tours around the country, like those gypsies who take midgets and performing bears wherever they go? Perhaps you might join them."

"Are you telling me that I don't have a choice?"

"You always have a choice," the King said. "You are a free man, of course, but I know what pulls your heart, Father."

"I want to fly for my own sake."

"Why this reluctance?" the King remarked. "We're not sending you into battle. We're offering you an opportunity. You say you are a scientist; well, here's your chance to serve science and make history. You should be thanking us!"

Bartolomeu looked at the two men with hesitation.

"What are the risks of this enterprise?" he asked.

Maupertuis unrolled a rough map and laid it out on the table. "The fact is that we don't know. From some of the tales we've heard, it's a harsh country. Our people have only ventured a little beyond Torneå, here." He pointed to a place circled with charcoal pencil. "The rest is *terra incognita*, unexplored and uncharted. Perhaps you'll find the bottomless pit there, where the sea falls into the earth, or perhaps you'll discover something so wonderful as to astonish the whole world. I have heard some yarns of this sort, but nothing would surprise me."

§

AFTER A day or two of reflection, my brother accepted the proposition. "It is settled," he told me. "I must go, not as an adventurer but as a man of science. The lure of the unknown is too great to refuse."

His decision did not come as a shock to me. "I thought you'd say this," I remarked.

"I want to sail the *Passarola* and here is my chance. It may be a folly on my part to take the risks, Alex, but what sort of life is worth living without a little risk?"

When he asked me to accompany him, the choice between a sedentary and an adventurous life once again confounded me. A scientific expedition was a lot less dangerous than combat, I thought. It did not burden my conscience. Besides, I had no obligations and no duties. I was carefree. In fact, it struck me that if I went away, my absence would scarcely be missed. Others would fill my space and I would be forgotten. With this realization, I found myself pining for manly feats once more. I wanted to run from the restlessness that the arms of my marchionesses had induced in me; no, run is a weak word—I wanted to flee. ℰ

# { 17 }

AFTER BARTOLOMEU received the royal commission, his lightness of step returned and the clouds of melancholy that had set upon him drifted away as if by a spring breeze. We made our preparations with all possible haste. Alterations were carried out on the upper deck of the *Passarola* to reduce weight. The ship was then lumbered with scientific equipment, warm clothing, fur sleeping bags, ordnance and stores. Great chunks of ham, cheese, salted beef, sea biscuits and sealed casks of water and cordial were lowered into the hold. Everything was lashed down and fastened tight.

In the final days, the King and many other persons of distinction came on board for inspections. In fact, Louis XV honored us with his presence so many times that we thought that he might actually embark on our journey with us. We were paid six months' wages in advance, with which we settled our business affairs. Bartolomeu received his instructions and gave a sealed copy of them and his will to his banker. When everything was prepared for departure, he and I wrote letters home to take leave of our parents. We were to proceed from Paris to Stockholm, then fly over the Gulf of Bothnia to Torneå in Finland, and follow the river upstream, making observations along the route. If necessary, we were to spend our winter in Torneå and make a second attempt at the Polar Circle the following summer.

We set sail from Paris on Friday, June 29, in the year 1736. It is almost sixty years ago to the day but my memory of our departure remains as vivid as ever. Children dangled from trees, women fanned themselves at the windows, men climbed on the top of houses and sat on the quays and bridges. An old cannon mounted in what is now the Champ-de-Mars was fired to give notice that the departure of the *Passarola* was imminent. The square was cleared, the chatter died down and everyone stood out of the way. First, a small globe filled with hot air and decorated with a scrolling shell pattern was sent up to gauge the direction of wind. Then the *Passarola* rose. The people cheered, *"Bon voyage! Bon voyage!"* as we flew over the squares and children chased the ship's shadow through the narrow labyrinths until it disappeared out of their sight. The feeling of the ship rising is something I cannot describe in words. Even after countless ascents, it was this moment that I found the most intoxicating. First the faces of the people below blurred, then the sounds faded, then the churches became indistinguishable from the houses, the streets became lines and the lines turned into patterns. As the air became cooler, the *Passarola* rose more rapidly. The patterns transformed themselves into craters and ridges and patches of color—green, ocher and blue—here obscured by a cloud, there sparkling in the sun; this transport from earthly cares to the sensation of the heart opening, the spirit soaring, was something that I will not forget as long as I live.

For the first four days, Bartolomeu and I kept our course north by northeast as we sailed toward the Baltic Sea. Generally we had a tailwind, which helped our progress. We landed repeatedly to replenish supplies and check on the integrity of the ship; we ate and slept in pensions and saved our food for later. Whenever we had a westerly wind from the North Sea, it was accompanied by rain, perhaps because we kept close to the coast, which had its share of squalls and hail.

To escape the rain and high winds, we climbed above the clouds. On the fourth night, when their dark shapes formed and re-formed far below us, we reefed our sails and remained at eight thousand feet. Bartolomeu boiled soup for dinner, while I remained in my cabin, writing in my journal by the light of the lantern. The sky was lit with a jaundiced light and Jupiter shone above the horizon, shrouded in yellow vapor. The cabin was not much warmer than the open deck. The thermometer had remained at forty-one degrees for the last few days but on this particular night it fell to thirty-five.

Progress was slow as there was not a great deal of wind, but the next morning a strong gale blew over Holland and carried our ship along fast until the forenoon. The vessel trembled in the current and at times I imagined its timbers splintering from the sheer fury of the wind but except for a slight rip in the mainsail, no damage was done. We kept our course by carrying a press of sail. When the sun

135

went down, we lay to under the jib mast and arrived in Kiel by night.

We moored our ship in a dry dock at the harbor. The port was a confusion of sounds, even in the gloom of dusk. Sailors calling out to one another, barges arriving and departing, ships unloading and sails flapping in the northerly wind. There was an air of purpose and energy about the place such that I felt the thrill of adventure anew and began to look forward to the journey that lay ahead with great excitement. In the morning, we brought new provisions on board and stowed them away. Then we untied the moorings. A crowd had gathered at the pier to watch the vessel ascend. We waved them farewell until they disappeared under the clouds. Then we drew the sails and the *Passarola* was again on its way.

§

THE VOYAGE across Denmark and the North Sea was without incident. The wind increased in the evening, the ship cut through the air at great speed and we fast left behind the lee of the land. We sighted the Swedish coast on the early morning of July 5, having covered about one hundred and fifty miles in the night. Flocks of gulls and albatrosses crossed the sky above us as we approached the shore. Sometimes they circled our ship and occasionally a bold creature would even land upon a sphere or perch itself on the crow's nest on top of the mast, plastering the deck with its droppings. With a strong wind astern, we progressed speedily, sailing at a height of fifteen hundred feet and rising to seven or eight thousand feet when the fog thickened. We traveled in this fashion for several days.

No two days were similar but if there was a common theme it was that we spent most of our time thinking about the next meal. We had to prepare our own food if there was no habitation nearby. Our meals were simple but wholesome. For breakfast, we made ourselves gruel and drank coffee, and although gruel is a food fit for the damned, drinking coffee on the deck, as we breathed the cool morning air and surveyed the horizon, was one of the finer pleasures of that life. Often, we prepared our meals several days in advance. If we were sailing over water, we would lay a net that trailed behind the *Passarola* and haul up salmon, catfish and bass at the end of the day. We gutted the fish, seasoned it with spices and ate our meals with fermented cabbage, or bilberries or raspberries when we could find some. When we were flying over land, we shot rabbit, duck, deer and pheasant and hung our catch from the poop deck to dry. We could not leave it out for very long, though, because it attracted flocks of vultures. Bartolomeu had a certain way of preparing meals on board by marinating them in rum, which made for acceptable fare, but if we made landfall, we put the ship down and roasted our meats over a spit. As we approached the Polar Circle several months later, ice and snow made it more and more difficult to find fresh game. On occasion, we shot seals and puffins. Their meat was good but the animals had to be butchered quickly as the carcasses froze instantly. Then the seals disappeared under the ice. It became too cold to hunt and we had to turn to boiled salt beef for dinner and soup made with fragments of insect wings and sea biscuits for supper.

All hands were usually required for rigging the sails, but we took turns in galley duties. We washed in streams and rivers. On warm days, we hung our laundry from the rigging but during the icy weather that came later, we washed rarely, I confess, and dried our clothes below deck. Finally, to our natural duties: this was, in fact, a simple matter. We had heads aft, like those found on a sail ship. The only difference was that our seat had a harness to make oneself fast from falling overboard. We occupied it only when flying over open fields or the sea; during the freezing months ahead, when we could no longer venture out on the open deck, we used chamber pots.

The monotony of the voyage had its own rewards. The entry from my ship's log from July 6, of "an enormous band of butterflies," brings to mind a flock of these insects stretching out as far as the eye could see. It was a mass migration of some sort, we thought, or perhaps these insects had been lifted up from their natural habitat and blown into the upper atmosphere. I had previously heard a story of a band of grasshoppers that had landed on a sail ship once, some two hundred miles from Cape Verde, on the coast of Africa. It was a most curious incident. The captain provided the explanation that the insects had been blown out of Africa to sea by a trade wind, but he ignored the fact that the grasshoppers belonged to a species particular only to the Amazon basin. They had come from the west rather than the east. I also heard from someone that in the midst of the Atlantic, their vessel had been showered with a cloud of dust, which fell in such quantities as to leave the entire deck covered with a layer of the fine, red substance. In any event, the shimmering cloud of butterflies at ten thousand feet left me in awe of the strange vagaries of nature.

For someone who has never sailed on a long voyage, the hours aboard a ship would seem long and tedious, but our tasks, the slowly changing spectacle on view from the deck and writing my diary left me not a single moment of boredom. I mention these small matters of our daily life because our pared-down existence brought about in me a feeling of fulfilment, of being occupied, and sustained a vague hope of permanence, a semblance of happiness, rather than the sense of ennui that I had often felt when I was earthbound. ℰ

# { 18 }

O N  T H E  morning of July 8, we arrived in Stockholm. The recommendation of the court of France, signed and sealed in Louis XV's handwriting, procured for us all the essentials we needed. While our vessel was being loaded, we strolled a little to stretch our legs and dined at a sailors' inn. There are countless of these in the sea-side quarter, all with low hanging beams and ancient stone floors. Ours had thick tobacco smoke hanging in the air. The fireplace was ablaze and the ceiling above it was covered with soot. Seafaring men gathered around long tables, drinking ales and throwing long glances at every newcomer. We sat slightly apart from the capering crowds, where the matron served us scalding stew from a cauldron.

The captain of a whaling ship also shared our table. A giant of a man with a flowing red beard, he entered into a long conversation with Bartolomeu regarding the undiscovered lands within the Polar Circle. Then he started buying us many drams of gin, which I found quite agreeable, and soon I was entirely beside myself. I found the greatest thrill in everything he said and laughed a great deal. He was much taken by the account of our flying ship and asked if we had ever thought of making a fortune. The King of England had a reward for any man who would find a passage from the Atlantic to the Pacific Ocean. There lay our chance, he remarked, and when he asked if he could be allowed to come on board our vessel as a crew member on our exploring voyage, I thought it was the most reasonable idea in the world. But my brother proceeded to talk very calmly, for liquor never affected him. He replied that although he would be very glad to take him, the honorable gentleman would have to lose a great deal of weight if he wished for the vessel to rise. The captain laughed heartily at this exchange and invited us to a long table, where his crew bought us more gin and related tales of whale hunts, disasters, shipwrecks and mermaids before ending in wistful murmurs about lost treasure.

On July 10, the day dawned with a clear sky. The fog dissipated early and the rays of the sun struck the sea at an oblique angle, suffusing the great watery expanse with a wonderful green light. It was a marvelous sight. As we left the wharf behind us and the shoreline sank below the horizon, Bartolomeu went into his cabin and left me alone on deck. The hours went by. The clouds turned red, then the sky became gray, the air still. I went down and knocked at his door to see if he wanted anything.

"Nothing!" was the answer. "I am comfortable."

I told him that all was well on deck. There was scarcely any wind.

"Very well, then. Take in the sails if it blows."

Thus dismissed, I came up again. My brother was always at work, sketching and recording day and night, in the smoky light of his lantern, the wick burning in whale oil. He saw the *Passarola* as a sort of ark. We collected specimens of herbs, plants and insects at an astonishing rate. He was always formulating new ideas and theories, sunk in a reverie, often forgetting my presence. Sometimes I imagined him as an eternal wanderer, cursed to follow the flocks of birds over the earth and to float between earth and heaven for all eternity, except that "cursed" is the wrong word—the sky was his true element and he would not have traded it for any other. Once I was in the open air, I threw down a drag net that I had purchased in Kiel and brought up a catch of small and slender hammers and a species of blue-tinged sea horses. I tossed the sea horses back into the water and slipped the hammers out on the deck, where they thrashed and snapped about for a long time.

I was absorbed in my own thoughts when Bartolomeu appeared by my side again. There was a gleam in his eyes, much like the one I observed when he regaled me with long dialogues on old explorers.

"Have you ever asked yourself what lies beyond the everyday sky?" he asked.

I was surprised by the question and remarked that I did not know because the abode of spirits and fiery comets separated the sky from the void. I said so in jest but Bartolomeu was perfectly serious.

"What do you know of Gil Eanes of Lagos?"

"He was a great sailor," I said. Eanes was a fifteenth-century explorer who unraveled the ancient myth that the world's end lay somewhere beyond the Atlantic Ocean.

"Every child knows his name," I continued. "Why do you ask?"

Bartolomeu fell silent, then spoke after a long pause. "Isn't it strange that we accept things as they are, until suddenly someone comes along and tells us that we have been wrong all along? It only takes one man to change our notion of truth."

I had half expected a remark like this and listened to what else he had to say.

Eanes set sail in a *barca*—a thirty-foot-long fishing boat equipped with one mast and using square sails—in the hope of rounding Cape Bojador. The cape lies on the northwest African coast and was regarded then as the end of the known world, beyond which lay a boiling sea, where the hand of Satan rose from the waves to grasp at lost ships. The Portuguese had sent expedition after expedition to circumnavigate Africa but not one of the ships had sailed past Cape Bojador.

Eanes was able to reach Madeira and Gran Canaria but as he approached the cape, the currents pulled in his ship and he found himself wallowing in the shallows. He decided to make landfall but the shore was ablaze with a mysterious fire and unapproachable because of the heat. At night, a thick mist descended over the waves; the ship drifted and a terrible sound of drums kept the men awake. When the sun rose the next morning, the sea had turned red. Fear gripped his crew. The soothsayer declared that if they went any farther, they would be burnt to the bone. Threatened with a mutiny, Eanes ordered his captain to turn the ship around.

According to some accounts, the Infante Henrique sent him out again and again to cross the cape but, overcome by difficulty and superstition, he turned back each time. The Infante now cajoled Eanes with rewards and ordered him to set out and not to return until he had rounded the cape. This time Eanes avoided the shallow waters near the coast. He sailed westward out into the open sea and when he turned around again, he found himself south of the cape. He found no trace of habitation ashore but as evidence of his feat, brought back clumps of rosebush that the Infante christened *rosas de Santa Maria*.

This was the account that my brother gave me. He spoke with great ardor, gesturing and rolling his eyes with the delight of a man recollecting a favorite tale.

"Do you know what the Infante said to Eanes? 'You cannot find a peril so great that the hope of reward will not be greater.'"

"And what was his reward?"

"A galleon laden with gold," he said. "But make no mistake—it was not gold that lured him. Look at the horizon—in the twilight it turns red like his uncharted sea. Do you really need a reward to explore that? I would go just to have my curiosity satisfied."

When he said this, it dawned on me that he had intentions beyond those of completing our survey and returning home. His circumspection so far proved to me that he had been quietly preparing a course of action. I could see now that his silence was weighing upon him and he was ready to divulge it.

I came straight to the point. "You wish to lay claim to cross into the unknown?"

He nodded. "The real unknown lies up there where the sky ends. I want to see what exists at the edge of the void."

"But we have no idea of what dangers to expect," said I.

"Why, you've started worrying already, Alex," he remarked, smiling.

147

"Will we be able to breathe? Will we survive the sun and the terrible cold?"

"We will be the first ones to find out," he said calmly. "Brave men spare no thought to personal considerations. Think of the old days when ships were sent out to find a passage to India. Imagine what their crew must have felt like, ordered to sail through unchartered seas. Storms, reefs and cannibals. Nothing to drink but brackish water and nothing to eat but food fit for rats. The fierce sun scorching their necks, the salt spray on their lips. The wind, scurvy and death always lurking beneath the waves. We have a good ship and ample rations. We don't have much to fear."

His childlike trust in destiny, a cynic might call it recklessness, won me over and I began to consider my service in a new light, where it required courage and valor, and the vanity, as I vaguely suspected then and certainly know now, of greatness lifted my courage and calmed my fears. ℮

# { 19 }

W E KEPT a northeasterly course. The *Passarola* usually sailed high above the sea because the Arctic winds whipped the waves and the swell was often so heavy that even at great heights, we were showered with spray. In four days, we sailed over three hundred and fifty miles from Stockholm. On July 13, we awoke to the patter of a brisk shower at dawn but a fresh breeze cleared the cloudburst and by nine o'clock, the sea was sparkling blue in the sun. We crossed latitude 65° 14′ north at around noon. The temperature of the air was at least five degrees lower than it had been in Stockholm. We brought out our sheepskins, with boots of sealskin and fur hats; and although the weather was still moderately mild, we wore these outfits as we approached the end of the Gulf of Bothnia.

Far away a white shoreline rose into view. We gazed at it through our telescopes. I shall not forget the sight of an armada of beluga whales, a hundred strong, their silver backs gliding through the sea, the gush of whale jets condensing into a mist above the waves. When the whaling captain in Stockholm told me that he had seen scores of narwhales swimming in the Norwegian sea, tusk to tail, I had supposed him to be raving, but I had never been so sober in my life as I witnessed this most curious spectacle myself. As we edged up north and neared the end of the gulf, we saw the first ice floes. Seals watched us lazily from rocks that jutted out into the sea. We descended to four hundred feet as the shore rushed up to meet us, and passed directly over the heads of these creatures. They were black in color and unwieldy in proportion. Albatrosses circled overhead and also present was a large population of small puffins, which waddled among the seals bravely, keeping their ground even as the seals bayed like misbegotten asses.

Three days after leaving Stockholm, we reached Torneå. This was a small, neat town with two

Lutheran churches and a school. The mayor received us in his house with hospitality and conversed with Bartolomeu in Latin. Many of the burghers were rich. Their houses were well built and they had silver forks and crystal goblets. The lesser ones had wooden implements, clean and perfectly serviceable nevertheless. I spent a pleasant time here, walking through the forests of pine and fir and watching the farmers in their fields of barley, oats and rye. Out in the open country, there were abundant flowers everywhere and no sound, except for the occasional crow cawing in the trees. We tasted their barley bread, which they spiced with cumin, and found it agreeable. Our few days of repose would have been more pleasant were it not for the green flies, which troubled us day and night.

After the sail had been mended and the ship stocked up with supplies, we continued on our journey. We began our work at the mountain of Avafaxa, which is situated some seventy miles from Torneå. Our instructions were to make a series of triangles by erecting signals on the top of summits and measuring the angles between them to establish the altitude of the sun. After erecting the signal on Avafaxa, we sailed to the next peak. Between the latitudes of Tervola and Rovaniemi, we touched down in the evenings to sleep on land as we found food and accommodation in country farms along the river. But as we traveled farther north, beyond 66°, 50', the settler habitations became more scarce and scattered. From Rovaniemi, our passage was filled with forests and deep rivers, full of cataracts. The weeks that followed were long and arduous. We toiled and we slept. Felling the trees and then clearing the area around the summits was no easy task. Sometimes, we had to clear only one or two trees to erect a signal but most times the summits were densely wooded and the air swarmed with flies. My shoulders and neck peeled raw from the sun.

We also suffered from a wretched diet. Fog hindered our observations. We had to wait for a distinct view of the signals and sometimes we were detained for several days or more for a single task. Then we bivouacked in the forest or stayed with the native Lapps. We had some difficulty in communication but an exchange of gifts established relations. Their hamlets were nearby and they would bring us dried fish, barley cake and wild berries. It was wholesome food but without garnish. We dreamt of delicacies and told each other of the fine cuisine we would enjoy on our return. I had grown a beard and lost considerable weight. My nails were black with grime and my clothes and hair reeked of wood smoke. Bartolomeu was no different; his cheeks had hollowed out and his face lost all traces of excess flesh.

The Lapps helped us because they needed the firewood from the trees we cut. They were small-statured people with jaundiced complexions and Tartar features who lived in conical huts. Each hut had two entrances and a vent for the central fireplace. Skins, stretched over the poles, formed the roof and walls of their habitat. In the evenings, they gathered around the hearth lying on fir and birch twigs covered with reindeer skin. The reindeer provided them with meat, milk, hide for clothes and leather and bone for making utensils and knives.

One day, their chief invited us to a hunt. The hunting ground was a forest that lay west of the habitation. When the chief, Bartolomeu and I climbed up the rope ladder to our ship and untied our moorings, the entire population of the village watched our progress. We lit a burner under the spheres for amusement so that the people could observe their chief rise in a chariot of fire. He and I went hunting. Bartolomeu dropped us off but declined the offer to come on the pretext of continuing his survey work.

We walked past pines, birch and spruce trees into the deeper part of the forest, where little sunlight came through. Occasionally, I caught sight of the *Passarola* through the treetops. It glinted like a solitary fish caught in a ray of sunlight before turning away.

The chief whooped with delight every time he fired the gun. Although his aim was poor and he wasted much gunpowder, he managed to shoot a reindeer and we transported the carcass back to the village, where the womenfolk cooked a meal on spits. Their work, their singing and dancing, all had an unhurried aspect to it. I became convinced that the beauty of this landscape, the harshness of this climate and the purity of the air and water all contributed to their unreserved nature. Although they were Christians, we did not see any evidence of Christian piety. They consulted their shamans for remedies and the name of Ibmel, their ancient god, was frequently muttered. The mayor of Torneå had remarked how several priests from his parish had had only moderate success even while living among

154

them. I met a few of these priests, married to Lapp women and living here like natives. When I saw how happy they were with so little, I could not help thinking that they had found a state of grace that our unwitting intrusion was going to destroy.

I was thus reflecting one evening when I caught sight of Bartolomeu measuring the sun's altitude with his quadrant. Rain or shine, nothing seemed to affect his spirits. I never saw him abate in his activity or reflect on what he was doing. I don't know what impulse came over me then, when I said to him that perhaps the arc of the meridian *should* remain a secret, otherwise there would be no part of the world safe from civilized man.

"A secret?" He started. "Only to be kept by a select few perhaps, and shrouded in deep, holy mystery? And you might also wish to render it a crime to seek such knowledge and burn those heretics who dare to trespass you? Ah, my dear brother, you remind me now of the same man who wanted to forbid us from flying."

I was struck by his reply but I was convinced that our arrival would corrupt these people and take away forever their simple life.

"Once we open up these parts, other explorers

will follow our tracks," I said, "and then will come more priests and the military and a garrison will be established, and then will come commerce, with all the vice that it brings, to burden these people with artifice and remorse and to cut down their trees and hunt the reindeer for the high tables of Europe."

"If we don't carry the torch, someone else will," my brother replied simply. "We cannot stop the march of progress. It will happen in time."

This thought dismayed me as I foresaw in it irreversible change.

Bartolomeu sensed my glum mood and softened his tone. "Only when we set out to know the world and unseal our eyes do we better come to understand our fellow men like ourselves. Why do you think it wrong to lift the darkness?"

"Because you talk like a missionary," I said, "and your faith in truth and the good of knowledge strikes me no different in its righteousness than the faith of those priests who say that man is born a sinner and he may only know salvation through Jesus Christ."

"Is it wrong to have a faith?"

"It is, if you think that only you know best."

He said nothing but a smile played on his lips—

whether of derision or embarrassment, I could not tell, but it was plain that I had dealt him a blow. I was inwardly pleased to think that his silence was a reprimand for my impudence although afterward, I was left with a residue of sadness. We spoke no more of this matter; the incident was soon forgotten in the rush of subsequent events, but I knew even then that we had reached a fork in our path.

Measuring eight or nine triangles had taken us over five weeks and we were tired. But this assignment complete, we could look forward to discovering the north. The Lapps saw no reason to explore this land where they believed there was no grazing and wondered why we should care to go there ourselves. Our questioning of what lay ahead yielded few results—spirits, an abyss filled with vapor, and ice—but I am at a loss to describe how splendid it seemed that we would be the first men to reach it. This was to be our own voyage of discovery to map the terrain and make an ascent near the Arctic Pole, where the void was thought to be nearer than at the tropics. I can only imagine that those early Portuguese sailors like Eanes must have felt the same way when venturing out into the unknown.

ON SEPTEMBER 12, we left the last habitation behind. For the best part of the day, we pressed farther north; by night, we moored our ship and slept on board. The Lapps had assured us that in the forests ahead, there were no large animals except for foxes and reindeer but we were wary of wolves and bears. Bartolomeu had seen bear tracks and the evidence was so compelling that on no account would he trust the natives.

For the next five or six days, we followed the Torne River upstream. Its surface was still like a mirror's, reflecting the silhouette of trees and the sharp jagged peaks, like ruins of cathedrals from another age. The breeze was light and our progress slow. We sailed over meadows and dark forests. Everything was shrouded in complete silence. Once, the sleek black head of an otter broke the river's surface. The creature watched our shadow pass overhead before vanishing below. The scene lifted my spirits and I spent the remaining night on deck. Although summer was past, the hours of darkness were brief. The sun was strong until eight or nine o'clock and twilight lasted beyond midnight. It was past two o'clock when I watched shooting stars in the dark-ening sky and the early hours of the morning when a cool breeze finally sent me to sleep.

Three days later, we crossed the invisible line of the sixty-eighth parallel. We flew over a vast treeless plain, a desert with bogs, shallow lakes and wind-swept tracts of scattered grass. In summer, I could imagine this wilderness to be beautiful but the ap-proach of winter had already stripped it bare. There was no greenery, only fresh snow and lichen, which was red, yellow and orange against the black boul-ders. The sky was clear and the sun intense for most parts of the day; but at night, the temperature fell below freezing.

On September 21, the daytime temperature dropped to fifteen degrees. We reached the source of the Torne River in the afternoon and watched as it gradually widened into a web of little streams and rivulets, flowing down from the lake. Its flow had become slower as we progressed north and here, it was frozen as hard as glass. Below us, seals basked in an unbroken line on the floes, their brown skins gleaming in the sun.

Two more days into our journey, we crossed the sixty-ninth parallel. We flew over unnamed mountains, unknown bays and unmarked plains. I felt that we had come to a forbidden part of Creation. The horizon was an endless expanse of ice. In the late afternoon, we saw something or someone moving in the distance. It was unlike anything we had ever seen, for sometimes it appeared white and sometimes it became invisible. We came down to a hundred feet and sailed straight ahead toward the creature. I primed my gun and aimed its muzzle at the moving shape but as we drew nearer, my brother came beside me and gently pushed the weapon away. What we saw were two polar bears—a large one and a small baby—running on all fours when they sighted the shadow of our ship drawing up above their heads. We gave chase to them at some distance until they threw themselves into an ice cave and disappeared from view.

Another three days passed but I felt as though we were immobile against the landscape. The same terrain that presented itself in the morning showed itself in the evening. Canyons of ice loomed everywhere and extended into the horizon. Was the ship stationary or was it the endless monotony of snow and ice against which our progress was maddeningly slow? We poured alcohol over the valves and the vacuum pump to prevent the apparatus from freezing. Our food had frozen to stone; even the maggots in our biscuits were frozen. Everything had turned to ice. ❦

{ 20 }

T HE COLD numbed us through and through.
We became insensible to refinements and no
longer cared about hygiene or what we ate or drank.
We pounded the maggots in our biscuits all into a
powder and boiled the lot in water from melted ice,
which we drank like a broth. We lit the stove on
board when the wind was not blowing but otherwise we went hungry. When the cold became unbearable, we drank rum to keep ourselves warm.
Half a tin can of rum early in the morning, another
before noon and a third in the early afternoon was
my usual quota. The rum burnt its vapor quickly in
the extreme cold and the liquor enhanced the senses.

On the morning of October 2, the weather deteri-
orated considerably. Dawn found us sailing toward a

wall of clouds, five thousand feet high, the layers stacked upon one another like the black stones of a fortress. It did not matter if we changed course because the storm gathered upon us from all sides. We lost sight of the sun. The roar of thunder grew louder and the ship began to shudder in the stiff breeze, which freshened into a gale. The wind changed direction every so often, or it died down and then whipped up again. The noise drowned out our voices. We close-reefed our sails and tied ourselves with rope to keep from falling. The *Passarola* shook violently. The jolts were so fearful that I expected our vessel to break into pieces.

By ten o'clock, I was overcome by gloomy forebodings. An icy squall drenched us completely. Then the snowfall began and the gale became so terrible that it was a wonder that our ship did not capsize. The mainsail ripped before it could be taken in but Bartolomeu did not let go of the tiller and by some miracle, the vessel remained steady. I kept the helm, the tiller held and the violence of the wind began to subside. By three o'clock, the worst was over. The clouds scudded rapidly across the sky and when darkness fell, I caught a glimpse of the moon shining behind their last, wispy remains. The wet deck glistened with its light. We furled our sails and decided to make landfall for the night. We touched down near a cluster of old huts, *njallas*, from an abandoned summer pasture, moored the ship to a rock and took refuge in the nearest hut. It was made of rock and sod and provided a reasonably comfortable shelter, although the snowdrift was like sand and it penetrated every hole. We covered the holes as best as we could and hauled in our sleeping bags, guns and food.

We dug a hole in the ground and threw in a bundle of dried twigs to light a fire. Bartolomeu poked at the smoldering wood until it was ablaze and then urged me to sit beside it, wrapped in blankets, until my toes and hands were warm. I was weary and my endurance was at an end. When I complained of pangs of hunger, he spoke of our mother's cooking, as if the words would magically transform our meager rations into her delicious food, and warmed a broth over the flames, sharing the watery meal with me from the same pot.

"Not as good as home cooking but it will do," he remarked.

"I miss home," I said.

"But why?" he asked. "When one leaves a place, things change and the place ceases to exist. The home that you and I remember only exists in our minds. If we go back, it will be like trying to fit into old shoes."

I ate in silence, letting it suggest to him whatever it might. If the place of my childhood had ceased to exist then where did I belong? Where did Bartolomeu belong? I was suddenly struck with the fact that my recollections of home were of a place frozen in time. If it had ceased to exist, then I could no longer return and pick up an old conversation where I had left it; my childhood friends would no longer be the same people I had once known; my sisters would no longer be girls I could tease but grown women with suitors and husbands. And what of my parents? They would be growing old with years and needing us. Suddenly I felt terribly alone. I would become like my brother if I continued this adventurous life, I thought, and I wondered what was the meaning of such an existence lived in splendid isolation.

"You should get married," Bartolomeu remarked as if he had read my thoughts.

"You want to get rid of me?" I shot back. "I am a burden now and you resent me for being here, is that what it is?"

At this, he raised his eyes. "Have I ever re-proached you?"

"No!"

"Then this is no way for brothers to talk to each other. If there is something on your mind, you should say it."

I said nothing.

For a few moments, there was silence. "I have been thinking about you for many weeks," he finally said, his eyes fixed on me. "It seems to me that you have been having certain doubts about this sort of life. It is not for everyone of course, and we must all follow our own paths. I just want you to understand that I do not expect you to follow mine."

"You are not angry with me for starting this whole thing?"

"What thing?" he asked, shaking his head.

"Well," I began, "had I not flown away with Maria that night of the reception, we might still have been living happily in Lisbon. My wickedness was the cause of it all. It was because of me that the Cardinal found an excuse and came after you."

"Why, good heavens!" Bartolomeu laughed. "I had almost forgotten about your tryst. Don't flatter yourself, Alex; that was of no consequence. It was the *Passarola* that sealed our fate. The Cardinal's summons would have come in any event."

My thoughts fell back upon his earlier remarks. "So what is this is all about?" I asked. "Why do you want me to marry?"

"I want you to find a soul mate," Bartolomeu averred, "and be happy."

"And what of you? You are not disposed to undertake the remedy yourself?"

"Who would marry me?" he asked, not dolefully but with gentle indifference.

"You don't believe in a soul mate?"

"I lack the imagination to sustain that hope," he said laughingly, "but it's a nice thought."

Then he passed me the rum, lit up his pipe and stared into the fire. The blizzard subsided, the hours went by and the fire began to smoke. He dropped off to sleep. I relit his pipe from the fire and watched the flames dance, dreaming of friends, warm meals and home among the glowing embers. Lapland had tired me. Although I was exhausted, my thoughts kept me awake. Duty or vocation—where does happiness lie? And where lay *my* duty and what was my vocation? My mind only stirred with questions. I had no answers.

The next morning, we awoke to the sound of the gale booming in our ears. The snowfall resumed and five more inches fell in four hours. The *Passarola* lay half buried under snow. There was more wind and drift all day long, which gave us no hope of resuming our journey. For two more days we remained prisoners of the storm, the gale howling around us, the fire blazing at our feet and our bags drenched with condensation. Bartolomeu fell into a black mood. I tried to cheer him but it was no use. Nothing could lift his spirits when he was frustrated and eventually, I fell silent from fear of quarreling, wondering myself when the odds would finally overwhelm us.

On the third day, the clouds lay low and haze covered the horizon. There was a pause in the snowfall and from six in the morning, we worked in three-hour shifts to dig out the *Passarola*. It was gruelling work, digging and shoveling the snow. We were bathed in sweat and I could scarcely lift my arms afterward but the exercise gave us ravenous appetites. We made a hearty stew of an ill-fated reindeer that came wandering nearby, and ate our meal while fresh snowflakes fell upon us.

On October 6, the gloomy weather suddenly gave way to clear skies. We raised anchor and sailed through a region of great beauty and stillness—a stillness that I believe remains only in the desolate corners of the earth. The nature of light was such that we could see cairns and rocky outcrops beyond the horizon. They appeared suspended in the air and vanished as we approached them. We saw a sparkling blue sea where none existed and glittering mountains, their tops flattened like thrones for gods, suddenly looming ahead only to disappear again. These were mirages but so extraordinary that we often lost our bearings, mistaking them for landmarks where there were none.

In the midst of the ice fields, we came across a hot spring. Its vapor trail had condensed into a cloud that we sighted from miles away. We prepared the ship for descent. The spring was of a milky blue color and its banks were covered with green algae. We washed our clothes and remained in the bubbling, sulphurous water until the heat had seeped into our bones. We were watched by a party of curious puffins, which greeted us with grave bows but muttered to one another, as if disapproving of our immodesty.

After a day of rest, we ascended in stages again. On the first day, we climbed through a shower of snow, plowed into the clouds and rose to nine thousand feet. At this elevation there was no wind and the ship was quite still but it was bitterly cold and snow and sleet, as usual, froze on our rigging and sails. The moon loomed over us like a large disc hauled across the void by an unaccountable power. Its craters and ridges were clearly visible. We closed the hatches and hunkered down around the charcoal burner for warmth but the cabin was nearly as wintry as out-side. I lay in my sleeping bag but even with three pairs of socks and my sheepskins, I slept poorly.

I dreamt that my body was magically afloat in the air. Sometimes, I would lose height but I only had to tell myself that I could fly and this belief lifted me up again. It was like one of my childhood dreams of flying, which filled me with joy and dread—joy for the exhilaration of flight and dread at the prospect of losing my magical powers. Then I caught sight of an apparition stalking me on the ground. Fear crept into my heart. I willed myself to remain afloat but slowly, I began to fall. I awoke panic-stricken. It took me a moment to realize that I was no longer dream-ing. The ship was plummeting to the ground. I jumped from my cot and scrambled up to the deck, where Bartolomeu was trying to prime the vacuum pump. I could see in the starlight that it had frozen over with ice. As we fell, the sail flapped into the rising wind and the ship started spinning round and round, faster as the ground loomed closer.

"It's no use," he said. "Empty the hold!"

I leapt down into the hold again and opened the lower hatch, pushing out the barrels of water, gunpowder and other supplies without a moment's hesitation. As our rations fell, the ship became lighter and our rate of descent began to slow down. At length, the ship became buoyant again and gently we put her down on the snow. All around us our possessions lay in ruins.

We spent most of that morning salvaging what we could, saucepans, tools, tongs, iron hoops, fuel, bread, coils of rigging and spare lines, and hauled them back into the hold. The soft snow had cushioned the fall and we were able to retrieve most of our things. We lost some powder boxes, coal, flour and the water casks. I was dismayed that these were not serious losses because I had secretly hoped that we would turn around at this catastrophe.

It took us four or five hours to prepare for our ascent again. We started climbing toward nine o'clock in the morning and rose steadily. We passed through some puffy clouds that were packed closely together like the paw marks of a cat. At dusk, the clouds were pearly white and they remained aglow long after the sun had set. By late afternoon, we reached the height of twelve thousand feet, where we decided to lay camp and sup for the night. The night was clear and cold. The constellations shone bright and there was not a vapor of cloud left in the sky. The temperature of air was seventeen degrees below zero but it was a dry cold, which made it bearable. Our hygrometer had never recorded such dryness.

The following day, we remained at the same altitude to acclimatize ourselves to the thin air. I worked at the sails and rigging. Bartolomeu stayed below deck. He had begun his observations upon the force of gravitation to establish if the weight of bodies becomes less at higher altitudes. At every thousand feet, he measured his pendulum's velocity. The velocity fell as we climbed higher. At fifteen thousand feet, the pendulum was moving slower than it had at sea level. Bartolomeu had to make a great number of observations as the air had to be still and the ship motionless. But now he knew that the force of gravity weakened as one went farther from the earth and for him, all the hardship we bore was worth this crumb of knowledge. ℮

# { 21 }

A s our flight gained in altitude, I began to experience strange sensations and vivid dreams. I recall lying asleep in my cot, and suddenly waking with delirious thoughts. I recall staring at the ice stalactites that hung from my ceiling and dreaming that I had become trapped within. I remember waking to the sound of ice floes grating against each other somewhere far below. It was like the sound of rolling thunder. At the altitude of three miles, the thermometer read thirty-two degrees below zero. I could no longer feel my hands and had to keep moving my toes and fingers to keep the circulation going. My movements became slow and measured, and any hasty motion caused faintness. I could not even write more than a few lines before putting on my mitts again—otherwise my scribble turned into an illegible scrawl.

After four days of gradual climbing, we found ourselves at twenty thousand feet. The air was thin and so cold that the skin from my fingers would tear off if I worked the rigs with my bare hands. The temperature was now forty-seven degrees below zero. Icicles dangled from my beard. The cold suffocated me and I gasped for air. My hands convulsed with a hideous twitching and my legs seemed to collapse beneath me. I felt that my flesh was being pricked by a thousand needles.

I was beyond my endurance. An entire day would pass without leaving an impression on my mind and then I would experience a few moments of intense clarity. I could see the edge of the sky, where the darkening gradations of blue finally turn black, and the stars, which could be seen at the same time, with the same surprising clearness as the sun, seemed nearer and nearer.

Flashes of light began to appear at the corner of my eyes, and sometimes I saw, or thought I saw, a dim figure at the periphery of my vision, only to look again and see that it was gone. I lived in suspense of these moments and awaited them with a sense of dread and awe. I remember this time well, as one might remember a vigil. And as I could provide myself with no satisfactory account of my experiences, I endured them as one might endure a haunting. My anxiousness mounted after dark, when my ears pricked at the faintest sound and my heart leapt at the vaguest outlines of shapes where there ought to be empty space.

The memory of one dark and moonless night still sends shivers down my spine. I lay under a pile of rugs and skins, wearing a woolen vest that my mother had knitted for me. It was tight under the armpits but I had kept it like a charm. I had hardly fallen asleep when I heard the noise of crickets at my window and perceived myself to be in my bedroom in São Paolo. I was sitting outside my mother's room. Seeing a light, I crept to the door to peep inside. A cross hung on the wall and she knelt below it, murmuring a prayer. A lantern was placed on the table and moths flung themselves against it. She saw me and motioned for me to come in.

"What is it?" she finally asked, putting aside her rosary.

I told her that I was afraid. She took me in her

arms and we recited the Lord's Prayer. Then she held my hand and we went out into the garden. It was awash with a thousand insect sounds but as we approached the grove of trees, the sounds fell silent. Everything was very still. I tried to mumble the prayer but no words came to my lips. I had forgotten it. Suddenly I heard a sharp, piercing cry. I opened my eyes and the awful sound was ringing through the ship. My hair stood on end with terror and I found myself paralyzed by fear. All strength drained from my limbs. I felt trapped inside my own body, as if dead except for a pair of darting eyes in my skull. Although a pitcher of water lay only a few feet away, I did not have the strength to fetch it. How long I lay there, I cannot say. I heard Bartolomeu call my name and opened my lips in reply but speech failed me. All I uttered was a gasp and even that sound died away. I rose from my cot and a darkness fell in front of my eyes. I tried to grope my way out of the hatch but lost sensation in my legs. The ship swayed. I fell and rose with a great effort, lurching forward to the ladder. Even finding a foothold seemed like an insurmountable task. I desired to let everything ebb away—the air from my lungs, the life from my body—and let the ship drift into oblivion. When I finally dragged myself onto the deck, I cannot even begin to describe the blackness of the night. It was palpable. I could not see even two paces ahead. There were neither moon nor stars but by and by, my eyes became accustomed to the dark and I saw the most magnificent spectacle.

We were flying high above a thunderstorm. The tip of our mast was ablaze with St. Elmo's fire—our standard, a tongue of blue flame. A scarf of bright light began to rise from the horizon, gliding swiftly up into the sky. It had its greatest width at the horizon and contracted as it reached the zenith, rippling along its cords. Soon the sky below us was also glowing with fiery orange and strange purple lights. Some of them had distinct pulsing forms, and tendrils, red and white, that extended up into the void, like the roots of some celestial garden. The sky was scorched red and we were being swallowed into a great, silent river of light. The river ran through the sky and surrounded us completely. Green waves rippled into the distance and thin crimson, violet and blue clouds, like strands of a woman's hair, pulsed through its medium. I had seen the aurora lights in northern France but nothing of such splendor. I watched the heavens like a man transfixed and saw among this wondrous spectacle fiery chariots, blazing stars and fallen angels.

Bartolomeu was staring straight ahead, both hands on the gunnel of the ship.

"Isn't it a beautiful night?" he remarked as he heard me coming.

I staggered to where he stood, clutched at his robes and fell to my knees. His face had a bewildered look and I wondered if he had also perceived something in the same air in which we moved.

"Did you hear that scream?" I gasped.

"You are white as a sheet," he remarked in apparent surprise. "What's the matter with you?"

"Tell me."

He hesitated for a while. "I heard a sound."

"It sounded like a woman's cry."

"There's no one here except us."

"What was it then?"

"A fowl."

"A fowl!" I laughed. "A fowl! We've not seen a bird for days."

"There's an explanation for everything," he said.

"Yes, there is—we are losing our minds."

Bartolomeu tried to reduce my fancies to the commonplace by reason and explanation but I was afraid, as any man would be, of sounds and sights in a solitary place. My mind reeled with confused emotions and the dread of a man who could no longer trust his senses. The moment passed but it was not long after that I was again confounded with ... I grasp at words to describe the wonder and terror, of what was, inexplicably in my mind, the sublime. ℰ

A T DAWN on October 15, a stiff breeze blew in from the east. We came on deck to watch the sunrise. A blue dye spread through the inky blackness across the horizon. It became a deep red before the globe of fire rose and turned it a blazing crimson. The void above us turned from black to violet to a deep blue. As the sun climbed up in its arc, we saw another marvel of nature: a dozen smaller suns, crimson, green and orange, rose alongside it, all bejeweled with stars in the fast failing night. The sky slowly turned pale and the breeze, freshening into a gale, scattered the clouds below us like cotton wool. The air was crisp and clear and as we sailed with the wind, the silence was broken only by the gentle flapping of the canvas.

The nausea that I had felt for some time now had become unbearable. I dragged myself to the ledge of the head and resigned myself to death. Coughing vomit, I stared at the earth below, not realizing at first what I was looking at—for how long I did not know. The ship swayed beneath me as if it were a baby's cradle. I lay there and imagined myself falling overboard and tumbling through the void like a feather.

Waking and dreaming, I then succumbed to a vision of a splendid city in the clouds—palaces, mansions, domes, spires and minarets, all hanging from vast globes and spanned by bridges that passed through the clouds to other similar cities as far as the eye could see. The city was suspended in the heavens miraculously free from the weight of matter, and magnificent in its grace. The minarets soared into the sky and were crowned with what seemed like teardrops of jade. The domes, of turquoise and cobalt blue hues, glittered in the sunlight. The windows of the palaces were encrusted with crystal and diamonds sparkled from the arches that led from one gate to the other. In the center of this metropolis stood a palace unlike any other. It was made of stone, white like the purest marble, and its arches shone as if cast from brass or some metal that gleamed in the

sun. Its dome was supported by buttresses that cascaded upon one another, moving upward from one
layer to the next until they disappeared into the
clouds. The entire structure was so immense that it
could have covered St. Peter's Basilica in its shadow.
The vision awoke me and for a few moments, I saw
the spectacle, brilliant and white, shining in the
sky. The roll of the ship lulled me to sleep again, and
despite every effort to remain awake, I fell into a stupor. When I opened my eyes again, the vision had
disappeared. The smaller suns had vanished in the
flaming orange twilight and the sunset had become a
single shaft of golden light rising up like a sword.

§

THE NEXT thing I can recall is lying in my cot. The
ship was descending. I could hear its timbers groan
and creak with every gust of wind, but I felt so ill
that I was barely aware of my environs. I rose and
slowly put on my woolen leggings and gabardine
blouse under my sheepskins. There was scarcely any
strength left in my legs. Grasping the sides of the
ladder, I climbed up on the deck and went aft, where
Bartolomeu was steering the tiller.

"I am bringing her down," he said, giving me a

sideways glance. His face was covered with a heavy scarf and his breath frosted the air.

"Are we going home?"

"No, Alex; not yet."

"There is nothing to be gained by going farther," I rasped. "The Polar Circle is death. We must strike south."

"We've not finished our task."

"The longer we stay, the less hope we have of returning," I said and tried to push him aside.

"Are you mad?" He shoved me back but I was so weak that the gentle nudge sent me reeling to the bulwarks.

I swallowed hard. "Did you see the city in the clouds?"

"What city?"

"You did not see it?"

"I saw nothing."

"Don't play the innocent!" I cried, livid with rage.

Bartolomeu kept a fixed impression. "There is nothing here, Alex," he said. "You are not well. We're going down until you get better."

"Oh, I am well enough, well enough to see that we're lost, lost in a land of mirages. Can't you see? Those mountains—they are not real! Those crimson suns—they are not real! Nothing here is what it seems. We're living in our nightmares and dreams. They've come to life and possessed us."

I no longer knew myself. I could not summon my reason. My ears rang with a whistling sound. I touched my nose and saw that my hand was covered with blood. I staggered on my feet and swooned from sickness and the loss of blood. As I dropped onto the deck, my brother ran to break my fall. He cradled my head in his arms and poured a few drops of rum down my throat. I drank the elixir gratefully but it was painful to swallow.

"We are finished," I thought and then I lost all sensation.

§

I BECAME gravely ill. My lungs ached and I was chilled to the bone. Then I started burning up with fever. Each time the fever broke, sweat drenched my clothes and froze them like cardboard around my body. Bartolomeu massaged my limbs with blubber but it only brought on a dull pain. I smelled of filth and disease. I lay in my sleeping bag, my sweat condensed into a puddle of slush that gathered under the small of my back. By and by, I lost all feeling in the toes of my left foot and several days later, I lost the sensation in my right forefinger. Fever drove me into a state of delirium and I fell into nightmares. My hands and feet were swollen with chilblains and I remember lying awake in pain and praying that one night I would quietly and painlessly slide from sleep to death. The end could not be far, I thought. In the brief periods when I possessed my faculties, I recall the flutter of our sail, my brother entering my cabin to assure me that we were not far from Torneå and his footsteps, echoing on the deck above.

I lost all sense of time. When I regained consciousness, I was weak from hunger. Bartolomeu ground a pound of flour, which he baked into a hard bread, as there was nothing else to eat. We poured a few drops of coffee from the pot and stared into the embers of our charcoal burner. We barely spoke; there was nothing to say. I slept in snatches and awoke thinking of food. When day dawned, we found ourselves sailing toward a succession of clouds, which were like dunes that continued until cloud and sky merged into the horizon. Several times we plunged headlong into the thick vapor, only to emerge hours later completely drenched and disoriented. Day after day, we sailed like this, making nine or ten hours on a circuitous path in and out of clouds. We could see neither earth nor sky. At one point, we found our passage blocked by an enormous cloud, a celestial mountain thousands of feet high, with gray foothills and blinding white slopes. The sun cast shadows in its valleys and the wind blew vapor from its peak. We began to skirt around its base but its flanks slowly hemmed us in until we found ourselves traveling inside a ghostly white corridor. Sometimes we would be looking ahead and a gate would open in the whiteness, show-ing the blue sky, and sometimes a gap would close be-hind us like the slab of a tomb. We drifted through this maze for a few hours, but it seemed like an eter-nity to me. I muffled my face against the cold. My eyes were heavy with sleep and I was convinced that all was lost.

I shall not know how we emerged. I remember waking up on a straw bed in a hut and faintly recog-nized the surrounds of our Lapp hosts. Outside, I heard the sound of children's laughter and the cack-ling of fowl and geese. The smell of wood smoke and dung filled my nostrils. A shaman sat by my bedside. I had not seen him on our last visit. He was an old man with a wrinkled leathery face, a wide nose and soft, broad lips. His eyes were set back in his skull like two dark lamps and his locks, jet black, hung down to his neck. His brow was creased with small lines painted with red pigment. Amulets dangled from his neck. He was murmuring incantations that sounded like a constant hum. Slowly, his hum saturated my body. My senses became so acute that I could feel my pulse throb and my heart beat against my chest. My eyes became heavy with sleep. Darkness came and then light. The past flashed before me. My dreams and memories merged together and became one. My ears rang with forgotten sounds. I was a boy again, twelve or thirteen perhaps, when I had fallen seriously ill. My father's remedies had failed and my mother's prayers were bringing no respite. I could hear people in other parts of the house, a carriage drawing to a stop outside, a horse neighing, my mother's sobs. I could hear leaves rustling in the forest. The noise became louder and louder until it turned into the thunder of ice floes grating against one another, and then it receded, finally turning into the flutter of bats, fleeing from the first rays of the sun.

I opened my eyes and stared at the shaman. He touched my forehead. I felt his coarse, callused hand against my skin and everything that followed from that moment I accepted without doubt. I became light. The weight fell from my bones and I rose from my body. The hut and the village vanished. I found myself soaring over a grand landscape of mountains, snowfields and lakes fed from glaciers. I was circling the tallest of the mountain peaks, crowned with snow. The sun felt hot on the back of my neck and the cold wind bit into my face but the height was restoring something else in me—an unbounded joy that was dissolving away the corrosion from every cell in my body. Now even the white mountains disappeared. The earth below me turned like a blue marble, laced with white and green and splashes of ocher. Then I was no longer flying but floating in a luminous ether. The stars twinkled with a brilliance that I had never seen. They seemed both near and far at the same time. I was fused with everything. All was silence and perfect calm. I do not know how long I remained in this state but at some point the ether started to fill with a soft murmur. The entire medium pulsed with its rhythm and the sound became louder and louder. Then the stars vanished. I lost the sensation of the imposing heights and was left with the shaman's voice booming in my ears.

I have no other recollections of my sickness except lying in my ship's cabin and watching a woman's face—or something that resembled a face—staring at me through the porthole. My brother was sitting beside me when this happened. He saw my stricken look and turned around toward the window, where there was a flutter of wings and the vision disappeared into milky fog. ❦

# { 23 }

I T WAS a cold and dreary November day when we saw the faint outline of Paris slowly appear in the morning light. We sailed unnoticed through the fog and set down the *Passarola* outside the Académie— an inconspicuous arrival on a wet pavement splat- tered with horse dung. I was struck then by the realization that this was our journey's end. Our four months of trials had passed, and despite all the suffering that I had lately endured, I was melan- choly. I regretted their passing. It seemed like years had passed since we had left. My memory played tricks on me. The hardships we had endured seemed golden now. I found myself longing for the smell of conifers and the stillness of the tundra again, the same places I had dreaded, and I dreaded enter-ing my apartment, the very same apartment I had pined for.

The voyage was hailed as a success. Medals were showered upon us and official portraits commis-sioned. An artist painted Bartolomeu dressed in the clothes he wore on the expedition—sheepskins, with boots of sealskin and a fur hat—holding up a globe flattened at the poles in his hand; the second portrait showed me sitting in an armchair, for I was too weak to stand. Voltaire wrote some verses that were added to a brass engraving underneath. For Bartolomeu, he wrote:

*Ce globe mal connu, qu'il a su mesurer,*
*Devient un monument où sa gloire se fonde,*

*This poorly known globe that he knew how to measure,*
*Becomes a monument which brings him glory,*

And for myself, he said:

*Son sort est de fixer la figure du monde,*
*De lui plaire et de l'éclairer*

191

*His destiny is to describe the world,*
*To favor and to understand it.*

We also accepted an invitation by King George to sail our ship to England. At Kensington Palace, we gave a lecture to His Majesty, the prime minister, the Duke of Dorset, various earls, the French ambassador and a posse of naval admirals. We described to them our voyage to Lapland and the observations we made, but most of their questions centered around the *Passarola*: how far she flew, how high, how many men she could carry and so on. During the tea party afterward, the King showed us sketches of flying men-of-war that he had doodled on the margins of a trade treaty with the colonies. The drawings were very detailed: each ship had a broadside of ten cannons, cast-iron rams shaped like horns and a double hull reinforced with armor plating.

"And what do you think of these, Father?" he asked, beaming. "I have drawn them myself."

"Quite remarkable, sire," my brother returned. "An armada of flying ships would do honor to your navy."

The King purred and looked at his admirals with eminent pleasure.

"I am sure that His Majesty has considered the matter of buoyancy," Bartolomeu added after a pause.

"But of course," the King replied, evidently prepared. "We shall fill the ships' hulls with hot air."

Bartolomeu should have let the matter pass but, never diplomatic, he did a quick mental calculation. "The weight of armor would require a hull as large as a mile wide and two miles long," he said. "Quite a large ship, I'd say."

The conversation froze. The ministers quickly changed the subject but the King had become sullen and once he became sullen, I was told, nothing could lift his mood except a little bloodletting. I had a fleeting vision of our heads being lopped off in the Tower of London but under the circumstances, a little bit of hunting was His Majesty's preference. The next day, the King boarded the *Passarola* and we sailed after the foxes as they ran down the estate and into the woodlands. We lost them in the woods and the dogs, instead of chasing the wretched creatures down their holes, barked at our ship. The King's spirits finally lifted when we took him on a pheasant shoot. He planted himself with a gun on the forecastle as we chased the flock in and out of

clouds, and remained there until the deck was car-
peted with feathers.

§

UPON OUR return to Paris, we began work to cata-
logue and present our findings to the Académie. Our
sketches, specimens of flora, charts, ship's log and
even my own journal came under the scrutiny of a
panel of experts. There were three members on the
panel. Monsieur Louis Lémery, the royal physician,
was chairman, and Monsieur Jacques Cassini repre-
sented the Paris Observatory. Cassini was included
as a counterbalance, since our findings rejected his
theory. We were prepared to defend ourselves against
his claim but the real danger came from the third
member, a representative of the clergy who was no
other than our old enemy, Cardinal Conti. I cannot
say how he came to Paris but friends told me that he
had left his post in Lisbon to hunt down Bartolomeu.
He hobbled up to us, leaning on his staff. The years
had been heavy on him. He was older and more
frail than before but his eyes still burnt with indig-
nation.

"So, Father," he said, "your great bird flies."

"For many years now, Your Eminence," replied Bartolomeu, "not only does she fly, she soars."

"Through the magic art."

"Through the grace of God, she shows us the marvels of the heavens and takes us to corners of the earth that no mortal has reached."

I wanted to ask for news about the court, hoping with vague interest for tidings about Maria, but the Cardinal brushed me aside. "Father, you know it is heresy to go searching for what is hidden and yet you seek these mysteries. Must I remind you of the horrible doom that awaits heretics in the world to come?"

"No punishment is greater than living in fear, my lord."

"So you agree?" the Cardinal asked, heartened.

Bartolomeu smiled wryly; "I agree that one must seek the truth in order to set oneself free."

The Cardinal became silent. "Everyone believes that you are dead," he said. "The Jesuits have raised your tombstone in Toledo."

"A golden city, with blue sky and green waters." Bartolomeu smiled with pleasure. "I could not have chosen a better resting place myself."

"You've been dead for six years."

"To be sure, some people would certainly hope so."

"The will of God will be done," the Cardinal snapped.

Bartolomeu bowed. "That may be so," he said, "but Your Eminence will be wise to remember that this is not the Inquisition."

§

FOR DAYS, the panel interrogated us on our methods and experiences. The inquiry took place in the domed hall of the Académie, where the panelists took their seats on high chairs on one side and a small audience gathered on pews on the other. Bartolomeu stood at the pulpit in the center of the room and in his slow monotone, presented his findings to the panel, until a cough from one of the panelists or a snore from the audience brought his harangue to a close. For all our fears, the proceedings went smoothly. Lémery did not care to ask many questions; he listened a great deal more than the others, shaking his head from time to time as if understanding things. Cassini also kept his powder dry although he could interrogate us like a lawyer when he wished and leave us floundering for answers. Only the Cardinal took bold stands and sparred with Bartolomeu, often digressing into metaphysics until Lémery intervened.

On the last day, Bartolomeu gave a description of our journey into Lapland. He described the terrain and gave an account of the aurora borealis and mirages. The mirages, he explained, were so vivid that on occasion we lost our bearings when landmarks hundreds of miles away suddenly loomed in front of us. Finally, he explained our method for collecting evidence on the theory of gravitation and concluded by saying that the results proved that the earth's sphere was flattened at the poles.

Lémery pushed away his papers and began to fill his pipe. "So," he exclaimed, "what would you say were the greatest hardships that you endured?"

"Extreme cold and blizzards, sir," said Bartolomeu.

"Thinness of air?" he asked.

"At higher altitudes, yes."

"Did you experience fatigue?"

"No."

"What about headaches, dizziness?"

"At one time or another."

"And you saw rippling cords of green and blue lights?"

"The aurora—yes."

"Fascinating, fascinating..." He mused and looked dreamily into the cloud of smoke gathering around him.

"Did the two of you see those together?" asked Cassini, giving me a darting look.

"Yes," I replied.

"What of the other experiences? The crimson suns or the flat-topped mountains?"

"They were mirages. We both saw them."

He turned to me. "The phantom city? The flashes of light or the things you saw or thought you saw? Did you both see them too?"

"No."

"What were they? Mirages or hallucinations?"

Lémery blew out a ringlet of smoke.

"I don't know," I said and doubted if anyone knew any better.

Cassini seemed pleased with my answers. He commented that much like the pearl divers who remain underwater for extraordinary lengths of time, it appeared that only men of a certain physiognomy could face the rigors of the thin air without suffering mental derangement. When Cassini and the Cardinal exchanged a glance, I sensed danger. The Cardinal looked meaningfully at Bartolomeu and taking Cassini's place, continued with the interrogation.

"Father, how do you differentiate a mirage from a hallucination?" he asked.

"Your Eminence, a mirage is there for everyone to see. It arises from the refraction of dry ice crystals suspended in the air. A hallucination only occurs in the observer's mind. Others cannot see it."

"Yes, but if you are alone . . ."

"Then you must trust your senses and decide whether you are perceiving things clearly."

"I have seen drunks who believed that they could perceive things clearly but we all know that sometimes one cannot trust one's own faculties, no matter what one thinks."

Cassini chuckled and laughter rippled out into the audience.

"I agree that the truth may be difficult to prove in some circumstances," my brother replied, his voice strained.

The Cardinal nodded toward Cassini and sat back in his chair. Cassini was now pacing around the pulpit where we stood.

"Do you agree that evidence—empirical evidence—is required for proof?" he asked.

"For proof, yes."

"Do you also agree that truth cannot be established without proof?"

A sardonic smile appeared on my brother's face. "With logic like that, one could argue against God," he said.

Boos and shouts of "Shame! Shame!" rose from the pews. Several ladies in the front rows swooned and a gentleman at the back pumped his fists in the air. The Cardinal rose, his thin frame shaking like a leaf. "Be careful what you say, sir!" he cried.

Lémery put out his pipe and looked grim. "His Eminence is right. Understand the consequences of what you say," he said. "Would you hang a murderer without evidence?"

"Truth can exist regardless of evidence, sir."

Lémery sighed. "But no one would believe in it," he said.

"That may be so," Bartolomeu replied, "but the evidence itself may not be true."

"That's a terrifying notion!"

"A jury may accuse a man of a crime, or"—he turned his eyes at the Cardinal—"an inquisitor may accuse a woman of being a witch and find evidence to that effect, but the woman may be wrongly accused."

"Father Bartolomeu is right," Cassini remarked. A thin smile played on his lips. "Proof itself is not sufficient."

It was then that I realized what was happening. Cassini had found a flaw in our method and slowly but methodically, he and the Cardinal had boxed us into a corner. The panel was now in a position where it could make only one decision. Lémery had also understood the tactic. All eyes were riveted upon Bartolomeu. Not a murmur rose from the audience.

"Father, do you have any confidence in the results that you have brought before the panel?" Cassini asked.

"I do, the evidence agrees with the theory," Bartolomeu said.

"But did it occur to you that the evidence might be flawed?"

"In what way?"

"You made scientific observations in circumstances when your faculties were under extreme duress. How can the panel believe them to be accurate?"

There was a murmur among the panelists as they discussed this point. A long pause followed as, one after the other, they each wrote something on a piece of paper and passed it to their chairman. Presently Lémery coughed and spoke.

"We need to verify the results," he said. "It is regrettable that the panel has had to make this decision but the noble aviators collected their evidence at the limit of human endurance and in such conditions as to make the degree of error not only inevitable, but also quite inexcusable."

"To hell with your regret, sir," returned Bartolomeu, shaking his fist in the air. "This panel is biased. The minds of your fellow panelists were made up before they even began their work. They won't lend their ears to a fair hearing. But you and I—we can talk. I must be allowed to fly again. You're a man of science. Perhaps you will accompany me as a witness."

"I don't have time."

"Then how will you verify the results? You need evidence. Where else will you find it? Only I can bring it, and I'll bring it, by God."

"The government does not have funds," Lémery said. "I am sorry, sir." He was the only one who addressed Bartolomeu with an air of equality and now he avoided his glance.

"The flights must come to an end," the Cardinal added, his face twisted with cunning.

"End!" cried Bartolomeu. "It'll end in this: I'll borrow the money and refit the ship. It is my ship after all. I lay claim to it and I will produce the evidence even if I takes me forever."

"That's bravely said, my man," said Lémery, "but the thin air can poison a man's brain, you realize that?"

"I've flown the *Passarola* many times," Bartolomeu sneered. "I know the perils of the sky better than the perils on ground, and you may lay to *that*, sir."

"I don't doubt it," said Lémery shaking his head. "I don't doubt it at all."

The remark seemed to cool Bartolomeu down. He straightened himself to his full height, looked at every member of the panel and then, gathering his cape and hat, walked out of the hall.

§

THE TRIAL removed any doubts in my mind that my brother and I had to part ways. His destiny centered around the *Passarola*; nothing could change that, and mine lay elsewhere. I had looked up to him, styled myself on him and believed in his convictions. His belief in himself had soothed my own doubts. I had identified with his vocation as I was too young to find my own and yes, my travels assuaged my wanderlust. I hoped that the voyages would serve as pilgrimages that would cleanse me. Each trial would bring its ration of misery or happiness so that with the stages I would unravel my masks one by one and finally understand my true self. But I was young then and preferred heroisms. This much I understand now as I write this chronicle—that I had grown up in the ensuing years. I could no longer live in his shadow. And this realization, once it dawned on me, changed everything between us.

I no longer felt like a little boy, following my older brother and hanging on to his every word. I felt what it was to be myself. I spoke to Bartolomeu as an equal and we spent a great deal of time together, walking through the Tuileries Gardens, browsing through old bookshops and sitting in coffee houses, talking about our childhood and our plans for the future. I felt especially close to him. I spoke a great deal, for I did not want to leave anything unsaid and he too was loath to leave my side—I don't know why; perhaps it was a premonition of things to come. ℰ

# { 24 }

THE NEXT summer, I bought a passage on
board the *Bonite* and sailed to São Paulo. My father was ailing and I had an urge to see my country
again. When the French coastline melted into the
sea, I heaved a sigh of relief and when the Brazilian
coastline appeared and the mulattoes rowed by in
their hollowed-out boats to meet our ship, I heaved
another sigh. I was parched for this landscape—the
red shore, the dark green foliage, the white-washed
houses. The humid breeze brought long-forgotten
scents and the shrill cries of the toucans and the
sight of banana trees brought back cherished memories so that for a moment, I had a fleeing illusion
that nothing had changed since I had left.

Coming home was like coming up for air. I no longer felt like a prisoner of language. Here, every-thing spoke to me. Every gesture had meaning, every tone a purpose. I did not need to explain my-self. I was accepted for who and what I was. But for all my sense of well-being, I was no longer my for-mer self. My experiences had altered me. I was ill at ease. I felt different from everyone around me and there was no one I could relate to.

When my father recovered, I thought of return-ing to Paris, but my mother begged me to stay a lit-tle longer. I had no clear idea of what I wanted to do and so I agreed. My father had aged a great deal. I felt saddened by his frail condition and took pains to spend time with him. Although we never spoke for the sake of making conversation, I learnt to en-joy his silences, and the afternoons that we sat in the garden, listening together to the cicadas, are my fondest memories of his twilight years. I decided to remain for another six months but the six months soon turned into a year. I tried to rekindle old ac-quaintances but I could scarcely recognize my childhood friends. The men I tracked down were like strangers. We had nothing to share. Our experiences were so different that we had nothing to talk about. I tried to spend time with my sisters, but even among them, I felt like an intruder; they were married and had their own families.

I missed the heights. My earthbound existence filled me with ennui. I searched for an experience that would give me the same sense of elation that I had felt when aboard the *Passarola*, but no matter what I did, I could not fill my days. In weakness, I turned to the bottle. I languished in the riotous bars along the docks. I swore everlasting love to negresses and fell asleep in the corridors of bordellos. I gambled for excitement and made plans to search for gold. In moments of desperation, I even drank the sacred brew of ayahuasca and watched my world slowly melt into a puddle of colors.

But I soon tired of this debauchery. The thrills were all too brief and the indulgences always left me with a feeling of emptiness. I was heavily in debt by this time and my creditors were making threats. I opened a small emporium to pay off my dues. If I close my eyes, I can still see my shop as it looked back then. It was a dismal, neglected affair, in a disused manor house, on the opposite side of the square from the cathedral. The ceiling was high and cracked, the timber floor creaked and lizards lounged on the whitewashed walls. I collected objects heedlessly—lacquered fans, silver combs, musical boxes, lace and timepieces, jet beads, plates from Dresden, ashes of roses and so on—and left them all to collect dust under the flyblown glass. I hoped to sell the business when I had enough money in my pocket but Providence had other plans for me.

The shop flourished. I should have sold my business then but instead I procrastinated and opened a haberdashery next door. As I cared little for commerce, I hired assistants. I was content to leave the affairs in their hands but occasionally I visited the premises to watch the comings and goings of customers. I was waiting for a sign, for something to happen, and biding my time.

§

ONE DAY, I heard a young lady's raised voice bartering over something with one of the assistants. I went over and feigning indifference, asked if I could be of any help. She looked up at me.

"I bought a timepiece from this shop last week," she said. "It has stopped ticking."

"Have you wound it?" I asked.

She twisted her nose. "Of course I have wound it."

"You've not dropped it on the floor or dipped it in water?"

"Certainly not."

She had a pretty, freckled face with a small snub nose and brunette locks that came down to her shoulders. An odd little frown marked her brow. I felt like touching it, to straighten it out as if it were a crease, but her large blue eyes dared me to even smile.

I took the watch to my counter. It was an enameled gold timepiece with a picture on its back of two entwined snakes surrounded by flowers and plants. I noticed a spring that had come loose and went back to the girl, muttering that it had probably broken in a fall.

My gloomy air infuriated her. "Well, you're wrong, sir," she said. "I take good care of my things."

"But of course you do, miss," I said.

I put the monocle back in my eye and pretended to examine the watch again. I could tell that she was a punctilious girl. Her nails were manicured, her fingers long and delicate. I wondered if she played the piano and inhaled softly, breathing in the scent of her hair.

"Well, are you going to replace it?" She had fixed me with a merciless gaze.

I colored slightly as I took the watch back and her receipt. "If you'd like to come back..." I said and started to apologize but she sighed, rolled her eyes and walked out.

My assistants told me that she came to the shop frequently. She bargained hard, they said, but this was the first time that there had been an incident. Usually, incidents like these bored me and convinced me of the utter drabness of commerce but this small episode roused my curiosity. I made some inquiries and found that the young lady's name was Catalina. She was the daughter of a sugarcane planter who did not live far from our house, in a neighborhood a little more affluent than ours. I was surprised that I had not noticed her before and decided to keep an eye out for her.

A week passed. I sent the repaired watch to her home address but she did not come. My vigils at the shop now became regular. I would arrive in the morning and spend the whole day in my chair, absently reading the paper or looking over the ledgers. Each time the bell rang, my eyes darted to the door.

I reproached myself for this fanciful obsession but when she finally came one day, my pulse raced.

She had come to thank me for the watch. I muttered some inane remarks and dismissed the other assistants so I could attend to her alone. She lingered about the shop and finally bought some lace and bedspreads. I made her pay a fraction of the items' cost. She saw the price tags and exclaimed that the things were worth a lot more, but I said that the discount was to compensate for the trouble I had caused with my faulty goods. She gave me a long, lingering glance and left without saying anything.

This time, I tortured myself by trying to interpret the meaning of that glance: had I won her over or did she think that I was a fool? I longed for friends to whom I could pour out my feelings but fearing that I would only be laughed at, I kept to myself and tried to forget my cares by taking strenuous walks.

I harassed my assistants to tell me exactly how often she had come into the shop before. They produced facsimiles of all of her receipts and armed with this information, I prepared a record of her visits. I looked for patterns and noted, with some despair, that her previous visits were irregular. Sometimes she had come once or twice a week; sometimes she did not come for months. It agonized me to think that she might vanish again.

What would I say to her when she finally came? And what if she came and I was not there? I devised elaborate schemes to lure her back. I stocked items that I thought she would like to buy. I thought of sending an assistant to her house, to let her know that we had received a shipment of the latest Italian jewelry—or perhaps she cared for French perfumes, which we had also purchased in prodigious quantities. In a moment of desperation, I thought of taking strolls in her neighborhood, in the forlorn hope of meeting her on the street and pretending it to be coincidence.

I feared ridicule and so, despite my bold plans, I did nothing. It was she who came to the shop again. This time, she remained for a while and showed interest in the new accessories that I had imported. I personally attended to her. Neither of us said much to each other and blissfully there were no other customers but occasionally a wretched assistant let out a muffled giggle from behind the curtains.

I learned then that she knew my younger sister. She was pleased by this discovery too; I knew because of the way she looked at me. When I told my sister, she went straight to our mother and reported that I was in love.

I was attracted to Catalina to dispel my own loneliness but by and by, I fell in love with her. She was of rare beauty and despite her simple clothes, she carried herself with the grace of a princess. She could be girlish and childlike in her whims but when we fought, she stood her ground like a lioness. She was a practical woman. My thoughts on life and fate exasperated her.

"You need someone to hold your hand, Alex," she used to say to me. "You have no ability to live in this world."

I hardly ever won an argument with her and tended to fall into morose monologues but, despite our little rows, she was interested in everything I said. She gave me strength. Her eyes sparkled with excitement when I regaled her with my adventures and at those moments, she seemed to me the loveliest of all women.

Catalina's visits became regular. Her tone also became familiar. Four or five months went by while these things happened. She introduced me to her parents. I trembled at the thought of seeking her father's permission to escort her, practicing the words endlessly and when they finally came, I spoke them mechanically. My years of wandering had not even taught me this, the most basic social etiquette.

Don Aquilino was a burly bear of a man, with deep gleaming eyes and a red moustache. I imagined that a scowl from him could send the meanest conquistador scurrying for cover.

"And what do you mean by that?" he rasped. "You've not even kissed my daughter yet?"

When he saw me squirm, he bellowed with laughter and granted me permission with a wave of his hand.

Whenever I went to their house, he was always sitting on the veranda, in a hammock, happily nursing a mug of beer. Catalina's mother, a small lady who carried about her the smell of lavender, told me; "My husband . . . he's a little lazy. He likes to sit and dream while his workers steal everything. He only goes to his plantation when we run out of money." Her eyes pleaded for understanding.

The apology was perhaps meant on behalf of their austerity. The house they lived in had be-

214

longed to Catalina's grandfather. He had made his fortune in gold and had been one of the richest men in Brazil. The old chandelier, the walnut settees, the cherry armchairs, all imported from Europe, belonged to another time and place. Everything was old and had passed through so many hands that the grandeur had faded away. The furniture was worn, the curtains moth-eaten and the sofas rickety. There were no paintings on the walls but an iron cross hung inside the entrance. It was a bright and airy bungalow though, and I was made to feel welcome whenever I went.

One day, Don Aquilino sat me down and handed me a mug of beer.

"I know your face," he said, lighting up his cigar and watching me with a squint.

"You are the doctor's son, yes? Why have you come back to this godforsaken outpost? There's nothing here, eh?"

"A man must settle down," I said.

He growled.

"I belong here."

When the tobacco began to glow, he puffed at it a couple of times and leant back, examining me at his leisure. "I am a simple man but I am not stupid," he

215

said. "You may have come back but nobody knows what's in your head now and where your heart belongs. You are not quite one of us."

"I am not a Frenchman either," I said.

Don Aquilino did not blink. "What do you want from my girl?"

"I love her."

"Everyone loves her," he replied, spreading his beefy arms wide. "The loafers by the roadside love her. The cook's boy loves her. The sailors love her. Do you think I will give away my girl to a sailor?"

"You doubt my fidelity?"

Don Aquilino put down his mug and for a moment I thought that he was going to hit me. "My friends at the docks tell me that you were a popular customer at the bordello," he said. "They still miss you there. You miss the ladies, eh?"

"No, sir."

There was an awkward silence. I felt very uncomfortable but I tried to keep my nerve.

"Now listen to me carefully," he said in a calm voice. "Your past is of no consequence to me. My own past is blacker than yours. It is your future that worries me."

"I don't understand."

"I know your kind," he said. "You have a dreamer's eyes. I want my daughter to marry a successful man who is going to make something of his life. Your type don't make good husbands."

"I will try to make myself worthy, sir," I said.

He smiled a melancholy smile and what he said next was barely a murmur. "Then you will only betray yourself."

Many years later, when he lay dying, he gripped my hand and told me that in his youth, he had gone in search of the lost city of Monoa, deep in the Amazonian forest. He took a hundred men with him and returned with only seven, all gaunt and foaming at their mouths, quite delirious with malaria. The men had starved. There was no game to be found and the fish were poisonous. Crocodiles snatched those who ventured into the waters. Others drowned in powerful currents. The survivors who staggered on fell to curare-tipped arrows that rained on them from the trees. They came upon a great uninhabited city of blackened stone and giant gold statues but no one believed them when they emerged from the forest. They were taken for madmen. The doomed expedition ruined him for life. When he told me this story, I finally understood why he was always wary of me. We were cut from the same cloth.

§

THERE WAS a garden not far from where her family lived where Catalina and I took our strolls together. It was a shadowy place, full of oaks, elms and magnolia trees. I liked the place because I imagined that some botanist had brought these foreign trees here to remind himself of home—wherever home was— and the palpable nostalgia soothed my own desire to be elsewhere. In its midst, near a lake, stood a white gazebo. It was so well hidden that even Catalina did not know that it existed. I brought her to it on my birthday. We sat on a bench and looked at the canopy of leaves above. Her knee gently touched mine. Birds hopped from branch to branch, chirping softly in the afternoon heat. Somewhere, a crow cawed.

"How's your father?" she asked.

"Not much better," I said. "I think my mother has worn him out."

"Does she still miss home?"

"At times."

"She'll find it a very different place now."

"She no longer wishes to be buried there."

"Where then?"

"By her husband's grave."

"Then she must love him."

Catalina was seven or eight years younger than I. She was lively and chattered about fashions and society gossip. I had little to say about these matters myself but I liked listening to her because her verve lifted my spirits.

"Do you have a wish?" she suddenly asked.

"Of course."

"What could you possibly wish for?" she asked, a wry smile on her lips.

"What do you mean?"

"You are a man of the world," she said. "You have seen so many places and done so many things. Surely you must have fulfilled all your desires."

"I could wish for simpler things," I said, wondering if she was not a little resentful of my past.

"What's simple?" she frowned.

"A kiss."

I bent toward her and kissed her for a long time. She let me hold her and remained still in my arms.

When she pulled away, her eyes were shining and she breathed heavily. She touched my lips with her fingertips and smiled.

"Have you kissed many girls?"

"No."

"I don't believe it," she said, her eyes searching mine.

"I haven't."

"Truly?"

I could see the disbelief in her eyes and I wondered whether I ought not to tell her about all the women I had been with. Then I reflected that perhaps she was really asking me to keep a promise for the future, not demanding an explanation for my past.

"Yes," I said.

I said so with conviction. I tried to remember the faces of my lovers but they blended into one another and dissolved like smoke. I tried to imagine the European cities where I had spent so many years of my life. The nights at the opera, the theater, luncheons in saloons and royal dinners. All those dazzling memories now turned gray. It seemed like an existence not entirely mine. The voyages over forests and tundra seemed like a dream. The sublime

feeling of flying with sails billowing in the wind—I
began to forget that sensation. A new emotion was
rising within me, telling me that my world belonged here. It was opening new windows within
me and letting in new colors and feelings until
nothing of my former life seemed real.

§

CATALINA AND I were married in the Church of
Santa Maria. Like most young people in those days,
we hoped to travel to Europe for our honeymoon. I
wanted Bartolomeu to meet my bride and I wanted
Catalina to meet him, for I believed that she would
never truly understand me until she had met him. I
wanted us all to sit in a saloon and remember the
old times. I had put a little fortune aside and our favorite pastime was imagining our grand tour, seeing
Venice and Florence, Rome, Paris and Vienna. I also
remember how much she wanted to sail on board
the *Passarola*. But then my father fell ill again and we
had to postpone our trip. A year went by. When he
recovered, business slumped and I became involved
in a legal wrangle with my creditors. I would have
gladly thrown my assets at them and sailed away but
Don Aquilino's beady eyes held me back. I felt pow-

erless. I promised Catalina to leave as soon as possible but another year went by. Our luggage lay packed in a corner. I remember how she kept packing and unpacking her little suitcase with parasols and bonnets, corsets and silks, always taking things out as the seasons changed and then putting them back in. It was unbearable to watch her like this. I could not even take her for a walk by the seaside without seeing the white topsails of an East Indiaman and falling prey to the feeling that I had let her down. I would have done anything to please her, and I promised her that we would leave as soon as possible. But it was already too late. Catalina was pregnant.

We had a son.

I doted on him. I had never imagined myself capable of such love. I taught him to swim and paddle in the streams and helped him catch his first fish. We fought fairy armies in the jungles and looked for old arrowheads. I remember his joy at finding a tree bark where a jaguar had sharpened its claws. A treasure trove of gold could not have made him happier. Gifts from his uncle arrived every year—an eagle's egg, a small model of the

*Passarola*, a peacock's feather—and aroused his curiosity more and more.

"What does my uncle look like?" he used to ask. "Does he have a pet?" "A tern?" "Where does he sleep?" "How big is his ship?" "Bigger than our house?" "Is it pulled by great birds?" "No? Then how does it fly?" Some nights, he would light a torch and stand in the garden, hoping perhaps that his uncle's flying machine would materialize from behind the clouds.

For his fifth birthday, he made himself a bird suit from toucan feathers and ran around the courtyard, his wings spread wide, the dog bounding at his feet, screeching, "I am *O Voador*! I am *O Voador*!" I remember that moment. My wife was playing a game with him. She was a great bird, chasing him and he was laughing, wriggling out of her arms. Now she was laughing too and as she laughed, I saw her as a young girl again, wistful, hopeful. I remember the rain too, a fine drizzle. I remember looking at the liana and pandanus flowers in the garden, nodding at us as they dripped with water, the earth bursting forth with the scent of damp soil, and I remember feeling happy. ℰ

## { 25 }

THE *Passarola* continued to fly. A year after the panel's inquiry, the King overturned its ruling and ordered Bartolomeu to return to the Polar Circle, with instructions to find the northwest passage to the Pacific. Bartolomeu flew along the Lapland route and made it as far as a group of unknown islands in the Barents Sea before heavy fog and violent winds pushed him back. His conclusion, that an open sea stretched all the way to the pole and beyond, greatly thrilled the King, but before Bartolomeu could be sent on further quests, he was taken ill and put to bed. He wrote to me complaining of high fevers. He was coughing blood, he said, but begged me to keep the news from our parents.

When Lémery told him that the Arctic air had probably damaged his lungs, he grasped the physician's wrist. His eyes bulged in their sockets each time he coughed; his rib cage shook like an empty cage. Lémery looked away but Bartolomeu's grip tightened—his knuckles white. "No priest for me!" he rasped. He lay wheezing and moaning for weeks. When spring came, the fever left him.

Lémery prescribed a spell in warmer climes. Shortly after, Bartolomeu received sealed instructions from the King. "Father Bartolomeu Lourenço is hereby instructed to set sail to India," the orders noted. "He shall forge friendly ties with the nawabs and find ways to increase trade. He shall do everything in his power to defend the interests of France, including taking all necessary action required against the British East India Company."

Bartolomeu stayed in Pondicherry for nearly nine years. There are various stories of his Indian exploits: how he bombarded the British fleet, his hunting expeditions and a rumor of helping an Indian princess elope with her lover. When French corvettes appeared on the Coromandel Coast in 1748, he and Dupleix flew out on board the *Passarola* to greet the flagship. But I mention these episodes by the by and only for the sake of completeness. Bartolomeu did not care for military or trade matters and followed his orders with indifference. He wrote to me, on the nawab's stationery, in sepia ink, that his sole enjoyment was floating over the landscape, like a kite. When he returned to France, his pension was terminated. For weeks afterward, he continued to wake up every morning to present himself at the court, only to remind himself that he had nowhere to go. He wrote, this time a bitter letter, complaining that the King had forgotten his promises. But the resentment passed. He began to sleep soundly and his spirits recovered. He loitered in coffee houses and wrote a chapter in praise of idleness for Diderot's *Encyclopédie*. He also made certain modifications to increase his ship's buoyancy, cutting down her poop deck, lowering her waist and clearing the deck of all other superfluous works— all paid out of his own pocket. In the spring of 1752, he resumed his ascents.

§

I DO not know what caused him to risk his life again. He said that he wanted to prove his experiments but I could not help thinking that he was going back for something else. He had found a personal freedom on his ship, unhampered by borders and custom, and the satisfaction that this nomadic life brought him was impossible to find in the cities. The sky had claimed him, and the vicissitudes of his life, the struggle against nature and the constant effort of dominating forces greater than himself, I thought, were so compelling that he could no longer turn his back to it. When I received his letter a few months later, it was difficult to persuade myself that I had made a better choice.

"Today I have broken through the last clouds," he wrote. "I was in great pains at first. The sun scorched my skin and the cold froze my blood. My respiration was labored and my muscles cramped, but now my body has become habituated to the rarefied air and the discomfort has diminished. I am beginning to take stock of my environment. Above me lies an emerald blue void, stretching out like an uncharted sea. Below me, the earth is like a giant marble. I can glimpse the ocean through the lace of swirling clouds. The shallows are shot with shades of gray and green and the deep water shines like a blue pearl. There is not a bird in sight. I am immersed in nothingness. Not even the wind blows."

Then I heard that Bartolomeu had risen seven miles into the atmosphere. The note came from Lémery. He reported that my brother had returned from his last flight in a state of delirium, with blood flowing from his nose and ears—and he wrote that he had seen something.

When Bartolomeu recovered, he wrote to me of the incident. He had seen a large bird circling above him. It was a solitary creature in the inky blackness, soaring at a height where no birds could possibly fly. He peered at it with his telescope and observed that its feathers were flame colored, its wings extremely large and its legs dainty, like those of a child but with talons. It appeared to be a female of its species and although he could not observe its face, he saw that it had a mane. The description runs for a page. He had no doubt about what he had seen. Even the physician's suggestion, that he had been influenced by an excited imagination or delusions induced by lack of air, could not shake his conviction. If it was a hallucination, then the detail is extraordinary.

I reproduce it here:

*4 June—*

*I have seen her at a great height. She glides through the air, wheeling round and round over my ship with the grace of an eagle. Seldom have I seen her flap her great wings. They must have a span of thirty feet each. She sweeps in large curves over my ship. When she descends to make a pass, she folds her wings and dives like an arrow but then she extends her wings again, gives them a single flap and soars. She seems to do these acrobatics for pleasure. As she glides over my head, I can discern a musky scent in her wake. Hour after hour, I watch her like this, wheeling and gliding over my head, all without any exertion. In the sky, which is clear and desolate at these heights, the sight of this creature is truly majestic.*

The next letter he wrote in his ship. Sometimes the handwriting is difficult to read, perhaps because the ship was rocking in the wind. It says:

*19 July—*

*She has begun to alight on the gunnel. On these occasions, she keeps her great wings expanded, instead of folding them, as is commonly the case in birds. She is cautious at my approach. Once, when I shuffled toward her, she flapped her*

wings and escaped but my slow approach is reaping its rewards for ever so slowly, she is becoming tame. Even the
noise of a gun does not seem to scare her. Perhaps she does
not know how dangerous an animal man is.

She is an elegant creature with a long and slender neck.
Her plumage is fiery red and extraordinary but the singular
aspect of her physiognomy is [illegible]. Her complexion is
black like ebonite; her nose is small, her eyes large and green
and shine with a brilliant light; her cheekbones are high and
her chin delicate. Indeed, the mermaid has a twin in the sky,
a nymph who lures the solitary aeronaut, kindred in soul
with the lonesome sailor all the same. Because she inhabits
the air, I shall call her my sylph. Watching her habits, I have
come to the conclusion that she is a most intelligent creature.

Some days, I am accompanied by her for the whole day
as she remains perched on the gunnel like a gargoyle, except that the metaphor is amiss; she is beautiful. She has
the singular habit of preening herself and then attracting
my attention by squeals and whistles. She can make pecu-
liar sounds which resemble articulate words. Is it a language? When the ship pitches in the wind, she makes an
agreeable cry, as if she is enjoying the roll. But where does
she feed? Where does she live? Why is she solitary and to
what species does she belong?

In his next letter, Bartolomeu said that he climbed higher than ever before. This time he fainted due to the lack of air, he wrote, and claimed that he would have died most certainly had he not been revived by the sylph. I have his letter here before me as I write this:

7 September—

*I started my ascent by climbing in stages. I crossed twenty thousand feet and spent several nights at this altitude to acclimatize myself. Then I climbed to thirty thousand feet. After finally reaching thirty-five thousand feet, I waited for the sylph. Two days passed but she did not come. I began to fear that I had lost her and felt numb with grief. With every passing hour, my despair increased. I resolved to spend another night in the rarefied air and fell asleep tormented by a foreboding. I saw her at dawn. She was coiling on the thermals, her wings spread wide and motionless—round and round she soared, higher with each spiral and as she turned, she called out in a high-pitched squeal, as if bidding me to follow her. I was filled with the extremity of relief and watched her spellbound. When I maintained my altitude, she collapsed her wings and swooped down; she made a pass over my ship, turned*

sharply and alighted on the mast. She fixed me with an
imploring gaze and filled the air with her flapping wings.
Her musky odor was most overpowering and even hours
later, I could perceive it upon my skin. But the next instant, she expanded her wings and resumed her ascent. She
repeated this performance several times until I was persuaded that she hoped to take me somewhere else.

I readied the rigging and sails, dropped ballast and followed her into the stratosphere. Ever upward she spiraled
and I after her. The sky changed its color from blue to pink
and the clouds gathered below me like a field of cauliflow-
ers, churning and swirling into one another. The temperature continued to fall. I do not know how long I watched
this spectacle but when I looked up, the sky had turned
black and the sylph was still wheeling above. I had been
shivering with cold for some time but now it turned into a
violent shaking. I was so short of breath that the effort of
taking in a lungful of air felt like breathing through water.
I forgot everything about myself, who I was and where I
was, and could not even coordinate my arms and legs. The
sudden motion of jerking my head upward caused me to
lose balance. Blood oozed from my ears and nose. I fell on
the deck and fainted but in the moment that I lost consciousness, I heard a cry. In all my life, I have never heard

*a sound that has contained so much sorrow and hurt in its heartrending appeal. It made my heart turn sick.*

*When I opened my eyes again, it was dusk. By some miracle, I was still alive. The ship had lost altitude. It was floating on gentle currents at around twenty thousand feet. The sun was slowly sinking behind a veil of fleecy clouds. Its rays had set them alight in fiery yellow and gold but I paid little attention to the scenery. I was just grateful to be alive. I thought that the fall was due to a failure of the vacuum pump, an act of God that saved my life, but the evidence was otherwise—something or someone had punctured the vacuum spheres. The regularly spaced puncture marks were like the imprint of a pair of talons.*

I was greatly amazed and troubled by this corre-spondence. How was the sylph so vividly described by my brother any different than my own vision of the celestial palace? I believed that he was imagin-ing her, but my conviction was weak. My true feel-ing was an odd sense of relief. I felt triumphant that he had finally experienced something similar to my own impressions and this vindication swept away my doubts. I began searching texts on zoology to see if such a creature existed. My search, furtive and untrained at first, turned into an all-consuming obsession. I trawled through libraries. I corresponded with Linnaeus and ordered the latest books from Paris. Linnaeus was composing a new edition of the *Systema naturae* at the time. He replied that such a creature would belong to the phylum Chordata, since it had a backbone, but since it had characteristics of both Mammalia and Aves, it was probably a creature of mythology. Could it be the last specimen of an extinct race? I wrote, but—irritated by my persistence perhaps—he did not reply.

In the meantime, I copied my brother's letter in longhand and mailed it to Lémery.

*"Quo non ascendet?"* came the response. "I have seen women who swear to me that the Virgin Mary appears to them on a golden cloud. I have spoken to men who cry like children, for they see demons gathering and crouching in the dark. Do you think I believe them? If their apparitions have material form then they must have some proof, some evidence of their existence, yet they have nothing to show me. Tell your brother to bring a feather, a memento. Otherwise, I am persuaded to conclude that such ravings are the outpourings of a possessed mind."

I wrote to Bartolomeu, and begged him to come

home. I copied Lémery's verdict and said that the rar-efied air was taking its toll on him; that he was seeing illusions and should abandon his flights. When he received my note, he responded in his old, neat hand:

*Vicomte de Turenne, Paris*

*July 3, 1753—*

*Alexandre,*

*People think that truth is something tangible, waiting to be discovered through proof. Let me tell you that there are boundaries beyond which proof and evidence become meaningless, language becomes meaningless and words lose their substance. Nobody can discover the truth. Truth is what you believe.*

This was his last meaningful letter. Something had come between us. We had less and less to say to each other and what we did say was so banal that it finally petered out into silence. In his last letter he wrote that Maupertuis was trying to persuade him to search for the southern continent. The King was partial to the idea and orders had been prepared for him to find Terra Australis and claim possession of it in the name of France.

The *Passarola* left Brest on August 4, 1753, sailing down to Africa and past the Cape of Good Hope and then turning east. After a journey of two months, Bartolomeu arrived in Papua New Guinea. He then proceeded southwest, along the coast of New Holland, before veering south. He covered an extraordinary distance over water and reached latitude 71° 30′ south. It was the farthest southern point that any navigator had ever reached but snow and icy mists hindered his passage and he returned without sighting any land. The following year, he made another attempt, hoping to proceed this time to the south of Peru. Some weeks later, we received a news report from New Bedford, America. The captain of the whaling ship *Nantucket* had reported seeing an airship over the Atlantic. He saw her getting sucked into a hurricane, and watched helplessly as the wind spun her around the vortex of dark cloud, faster and faster—her sails torn, her mast ripped and the hull disintegrating—propelling her ever upward into the eye of the storm until the ship disappeared from sight. This was the last sighting of the *Passarola*, near Cape Verde, heading south by southwest and bearing homeward. ૭

# { 26 }

A LL THIS happened a long, long time ago. The *Passarola* is lost and most people have forgotten Bartolomeu. His portrait and records perished in the sack of Versailles. The Revolutionaries burnt everything. Voltaire's verses are now entirely attributed to Maupertuis. The old Lisbon no longer exists. Its inhabitants and their memories lie buried under a new military town with battlements, towers and bays. I traveled there once for old time's sake and found myself a stranger. Even in Paris, the old people are gone and the haunts of our youth are vanishing. The new people have become fond of spectacle, so the music is noise and the opera is without charm. The skies are dotted with Montgolfier balloons. In the streets, the children, instead of playing with

hoops and sticks, salute one another. There is a constant clamor of things, a formless noise, which, I
fear, hides the rumble of cannons.

My father died many years ago. My mother, bless
her, has also passed away. She lived to a very old age,
in the same house where we were born. I have fond
memories of the place and they were rekindled each
time I visited her—hot stew, the smell of jasmine
and the song of cicadas in the late afternoon. But I
found that the more time passed, the more she
clutched at her past. She draped the old furniture
with white sheets, which, like shrouds, protected it
from dust. She kept our childhood rooms like they
used to be when we were young. She also kept all of
Bartolomeu's letters in a silver chest. They had yellowed with age but she would not part with them.
She read them every so often and after reading them,
she would fold them neatly and put them away.
Every day, she opened the windows of his boyhood
room to let the fresh air in. She kept his clothes, an-
tiquated and moth-eaten, in trunks. In her mind, his
image never grew old. "He is a young man now," she
used to tell me, "no longer a boy. When will he put a
stop to his flights and settle down like everyone
else? He should be out in the company of other

young men, going hunting, shooting, visiting respectable saloons, escorting ladies to the balls, if he
must, but he must stop this madness."

Madness . . . I no longer even know what this
word means. I long ago stopped asking such questions, for at my age I have no beliefs. I have seen too
many things to have any faith. My time is past. I
don't even know who I am and what I have lived for.
I have been a father, a husband, a good citizen—yes;
but is that all there is to life? I confess that with my
family around me, my desire to travel wore away.
My ambition was satisfied by my business affairs
and by and by, I lost the restlessness of my youth. I
was respected and with that, I became content. But
when I look back upon my life, I feel like an actor after the curtain has fallen, the applause has died
away and everyone has walked off the stage. I feel a
deep emptiness inside. I chose a life of comfort but
part of me always longed for adventure. I remember
my childhood and youth as clearly as the light of
day but the last week, the last year, the last decade—
they have all vanished in a blur. I cannot help but
think how it all might have turned out had I never
come home. I feel that my hankering for respectabil-
ity, for settling down like mud, was in fact nothing

239

but cowardice that kept me from living a full life. I feel that when I stifled the restlessness of my youth I also let a part of myself die.

It is too late now. I am an old man. Old age is not unhappy but it brings with it its own loneliness. I am tormented by my memories and sometimes, I am assuaged by them. The careless sleep of youth eludes me. I suffer from a recurring dream that I have become a shadow. People I know pass me by. I walk on a boulevard but I cannot enter any buildings. Doors that were open to me are now shut. I wake up gasping for air. I twist and turn in bed. I whisper the names of my childhood friends. When it rains, the moist soil brings to me fragrances long forgotten. There are nights when I hear the clatter of a carriage downstairs. I hear the sound of glasses tinkling and laughter spilling out into the dark. I fling open my window to see who is out there. But the night is black. There is only the silent rustle of the forest. I fall back into my fitful sleep. But close to the summer solstice, when the sky is clear and a deep hush falls over the forest, I lie awake in my bed and wait for another sound—a solitary wail that comes from deep within the sky. It is this cry that reminds me of my brother.

# *Author's Note*

THE Brazilian-born priest Bartolomeu Lourenço de Gusmão is regarded as a pioneer in aviation history. He was one of twelve children born to a doctor and his wife, Francisco and Marie Alvares Lourenço. After completing his early studies at Bahia, Bartolomeu sailed for Portugal in 1705, where he began working on the concept of a flying ship, which he called the *Passarola* (great bird). A number of paintings and drawings from the period suggest that it was hybrid of a balloon and a glider, but the exact size and design of the craft is unknown. There is also no reliable evidence to suggest that it ever carried human cargo. However, Bartolomeu's first practical demonstration of a flying model before the Court on August 8, 1709, precedes the Montgolfier hot air balloon by over seventy years. Bartolomeu's experiments drew wide praise but also attracted the attention of the Inquisition. When he fell out of favor with the King, he was warned that the Inquisition was going to arrest and have him tried on charges of sorcery. He fled to Spain, where he died of fever in Toledo in 1724. He was 39 years old.

The adventures of Bartolomeu and his brother in this novel, both real historical figures, are ficti-tious. ℰ